"I know you. I know who you are and what you're capable of."

She jingled the cuffs. "If you want any more information out of me, hold out your arm—your right arm."

He stretched his arm in front of him. Two more inches and he could touch her soft cheek, tell her everything he'd thought about this past year.

She snapped the cuff around his wrist and yanked on it, the metal cutting into his flesh. "Over here, by the radiator."

He would've preferred the bedroom, but he followed in her wake as she pulled him toward the window.

"Rikki, I'd never hurt you."

"You were singing a different tune sixteen months ago."

BULLETPROOF SEAL

CAROL ERICSON

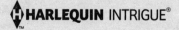

ISBN-13: 978-1-335-52624-3

Bulletproof SEAL

Copyright © 2018 by Carol Ericson

Printed in U.S.A.

Carol Ericson is a bestselling, award-winning author of more than forty books. She has an eerie fascination for true-crime stories, a love of film noir and a weakness for reality TV, all of which fuel her imagination to create her own tales of murder, mayhem and mystery. To find out more about Carol and her current projects, please visit her website at www.carolericson.com, "where romance flirts with danger."

CAST OF CHARACTERS

Rikki Taylor—A CIA agent who was captured in North Korea, she's now free with a different identity. She's ready to track down the people who set her up—including her navy SEAL lover, who had her in his crosshairs with orders to take her out.

Quinn McBride—Racked with guilt and remorse for playing a role in the North Koreans' capture of Rikki, this navy SEAL sniper will do anything in his power to protect her...and the baby he never knew they had.

Jeff Banks—A CIA agent on a mission to pass information to Rikki, although he doesn't know her true identity...or does he?

David Dawson—Rikki's partner and CIA mentor died on their mission to North Korea, but he may not have been completely honest with Rikki about the nature of that mission.

Belinda Dawson—David's wife may know more than she's willing to admit, because what she knows just might end up killing her.

Frederick Von—David's contact for the secret mission to North Korea. He also shares a name with a traitorous character in David's novel, which may or may not be a coincidence.

Vlad—A sniper for the insurgents during the Gulf War. He has been assembling an international terrorist network that has infiltrated United States security agencies, but his luck may have run out when he finally meets his match.

Ariel—The mysterious head of the Vlad task force, Ariel is now ready to reveal her identity in order to take out the enemy...and it's personal.

Prologue

The sweat stung Quinn's eyes and he squeezed them shut for a second—just a second before he refocused on his target. Rikki's beautiful face swam before him in his scope, her red hair standing out like a burst of flame against the emerald green landscape. Quinn's hand trembled.

He shifted his sniper rifle to the two North Korean soldiers walking behind Rikki, prodding her forward. They had rifles pointed at her back. Quinn spit the sour taste out of his mouth, along with the mud from the hillside in the DMZ between North and South Korea.

Someone had misinformed the CIA. Rikki Taylor was no rogue operative working with the North Koreans. She was their captive...unless she'd set up this whole scene for cover.

Quinn knew better than anyone about Rikki's duplicitous nature. But this? Working with the enemy to damage her own government and put her fellow CIA agents at risk?

He had a hard time believing Rikki would endanger agents in the field. Quinn lowered his sniper rifle and swiped the back of his hand across his mouth.

The trio below him stopped, and one of the soldiers pulled out a bottle of water.

Squinting, Quinn scanned the lush land where the borders of North and South Korea met—a no-man's-land where hostility and mistrust haunted the verdant beauty—not to mention the scattered land mines. This mistrust permeated his pores, had him doubting his mission, a mission he should've refused once he'd discovered the target.

He would've had to have come up with a good reason to refuse an assignment from the navy—even after that untraceable text he'd received. He could've tried the truth, but then he would've come under suspicion. Then his pride had taken over and he had to prove that he could carry out the assignment, prove his professionalism and dedication.

He snorted softly, and the leaves on the branch tickling his nose stirred. Prove to whom? His old man?

The group on the ground was on the move again, and Quinn took up his position. His rifle weighed on his shoulder like a lead block. His breath came out in short spurts.

Usually before he dropped a target, a deadly calm descended on him. Now, his heart raced and his trigger finger twitched. In this condition he'd be lucky to hit that boulder twenty feet away.

He closed his eyes and took a deep, steadying breath through his nose and blew it out through puckered lips. He swallowed. He shifted. He braced the toes of his boots against the rock behind him.

Then he refocused. He put Rikki Taylor in his crosshairs for the last time.

Rikki licked her lips, and Quinn could almost taste their sweet honey on his own tongue. She tossed her fiery hair over one shoulder.

Quinn blinked and, in the split second of that one blink, Rikki attacked one of the guards, going for his weapon.

Quinn needed no other proof. He tracked his rifle to the other guard, lined him up and took the shot. The soldier jerked once and dropped to the ground.

Quinn swung his scope back to Rikki's struggle with her captor, and his heart stuttered. The soldier had possession of his gun, and Rikki had fallen to the ground, out of sight behind a clump of bushes.

As Quinn watched through his scope, blood pounding in his ears, the North Korean soldier shot his weapon into the bushes.

In a fury, Quinn zeroed in on the man who'd just shot Rikki, but before he could even take aim, Quinn came under attack from a hail of bullets.

Taking down the other soldier had revealed his position, and now he was outnumbered and outgunned. He rolled to his back and scrambled down the hillside like a forward-moving crab. He scuttled behind a row of trees and started breaking down his rifle.

Dragging himself up and wedging his back against a tree trunk, he stuffed his gear into his bag and then swung it onto his back.

He lunged forward onto his belly and army-crawled his way through the forest to the tunnel that would take him back to South Korea and the designated pickup point.

What would he tell his superiors? He did end up with mission success. Although it wasn't his bullet that had done the job, he *had* neutralized the target—Rikki Taylor.

They'd been wrong. They'd all been wrong. Rikki had not been working with the enemy.

And now that Quinn was responsible for her death, his life wasn't worth living.

Chapter One

Sixteen months later

The footsteps echoed behind her on the rain-slicked pavement. Rikki stopped and spun around. Silence greeted her as she peered down the dark, narrow street.

With her muscles coiled tightly, she continued, and her tag-along followed suit. As she began to turn again, the footsteps, two sets, quickened and two bodies rushed her.

The glint from a knife flashed in the night, and Rikki finished her turn with her feet flying. She kicked the assailant with the knife in the gut, and he doubled over, his weapon clattering to the cobble-stones.

The other man yelped in surprise and before he could recover, Rikki swept up the knife from the ground and wielded it toward her attacker's face.

"Get lost, or I'll slice you from chin to navel. Yu done know?"

The man's eyes widened so that the whites gleamed like two orbs. His friend groaned from the ground.

Rikki growled, "And take him with you."

He held up one hand and grabbed his buddy by the arm with the other, dragging him to his feet. "Eazy, nuh."

"You take it easy and get moving or I'll call the police."

The two hapless muggers took off, and Rikki pocketed the knife. The streets of Jamaica, even in the tourist trap of Montego Bay, turned deadly after dark, but Rikki had more to fear in her own country right now.

She slipped into the alley where an orange light swayed in the breeze, sidling along the walls of the ramshackle building. She ducked under a tattered blue-and-white-striped awning and rapped at the window.

A curtain stirred. Rikki stepped sideways into the weak light to identify herself.

A wiry man opened the door and hustled her inside as he poked his head into the alley and looked both ways. "Where's your ride?"

"I walked from the main street."

He shook his head. "Dangerous place for anyone to be walking, especially a girl like you."

Rikki hid her smile behind a covered cough. "I'm okay. Are you Baily?"

"The one and only." He double-locked the door behind them and twitched the curtain back in place.

"Do you have everything ready?"

"Come with me." He crooked one long finger in her direction.

Rikki followed him through a single room where an old woman sat in front of an older TV, the blue light flickering across her lined face. She didn't acknowledge Rikki's presence or even move a muscle.

Baily shoved a dark curtain aside and waved Rikki into a small room. He pointed to a green screen and said, "Stand in front of that. I'll get your picture first. Everything else is ready to go."

As she took a step toward the screen, Baily tugged on her sleeve. "Business first."

Rikki pulled a wad of cash from her pocket. Those thieves on the street would've hit pay dirt with her— well, except for the fact that they'd picked a CIA operative, trained in self-defense and street fighting, as their target.

She counted out the agreed-upon sum, and Baily got to work.

Thirty minutes later, Rikki had a Canadian passport and a birth certificate for one April Thompson. She studied the passport with the Jamaican stamp. "I heard you were good, Baily. These better not let me down."

"Never had a problem yet." He cocked his head in a birdlike fashion. "Girl like you in trouble with the Babylon?"

"Babylon?" She stuffed the documents into the manila envelope he'd handed to her.

"De law." He waved his hands in a big circle. "De system."

"You could say that." She stuck out her hand. "Pleasure doing business with you."

He shook her hand and then yelled, "Darien!"

Rikki jumped, jerking her hand from his grip and placing it over the newly acquired knife in her waistband.

Baily placed one finger against the side of his nose. "No worries. Darien just my boy. He'll take you back."

A skinny young man poked his head into the room, his dreadlocks bobbing and swaying. "Yeah, Daddy?"

"Take this young woman wherever she wants to go. Don't stop anywhere."

Darien grinned. "Sure ting."

After thanking Baily, Rikki followed Darien outside.

He turned sideways and scooted between two of the houses along the alley. A chain clinked and rattled, and Darien pushed a scooter out in front of him. "Hop on de back."

Clutching her fake documents to her chest, Rikki climbed on the back of Darien's scooter. He zoomed through the streets of Montego Bay as she shouted directions in his ear over the buzzing sound of the bike.

A block away from the resort, she tapped Darien's shoulder and pointed to the side of the street.

The bike sputtered to a stop, and he leaned it to one side as if it were a mammoth Harley instead of a putt-putt scooter. Rikki slid off the back and handed Darien a folded bill.

His gaze darted from the outstretched money to her face. "Daddy would smack me in da head if I took that."

"Daddy doesn't have to know." She tucked the cash beneath his fingers curled around the handlebar of his scooter and twirled away. She made a beeline for the resort and didn't slow her pace until she walked through the front entrance.

"Good evening, Miss Rikki."

"Hey, George." She waved her manila envelope and scurried out the side door and across the pool deck, where drunken tourists had gathered for one last nightcap.

The damp foliage brushed her skin, and she inhaled the sweet, heavy fragrance of the white bellflower as she tromped down the path to the cottage. When she was inside, she leaned against the front door, closing her eyes and hugging the fake documents to her chest.

"Did you get what you needed, Rikki?"

Rikki opened one eye and dipped her chin to her chest. "I did. Thanks, Chaz."

Her stepfather winked. "I've been on this island a long time. I know important people in low places."

Her mother floated into the room behind Chaz, her long gray braid hanging over one shoulder. "Are you sure you want to do this, Rikki? You don't owe them anything, and as far as they know, you're dead.

You and Bella could live here with us for as long as you like."

Rikki rolled her eyes. "I would go stir-crazy here, Mom. Besides, I have to do this. I have important information."

"They don't deserve it." Mom sniffed.

Bella cooed and gurgled from the other room, and Rikki dropped the manila envelope on a table and hurried toward the bedroom. She leaned over the crib and scooped up her baby girl, holding her close and breathing in her baby-powder scent.

"She's going to miss you."

Rikki glanced at her mom, who stood with her shoulder wedged against the doorjamb, and blinked the sudden tears from her eyes. "I'm doing it for her, Mom. I have to get my life back for both of us."

"Does that mean seeing *him*?"

"I have to start with him, see what he knows, maybe use his contacts."

"You don't have to tell him about Bella. She'll be safe with us until you can return and reclaim her, reclaim your life."

Rikki bounced her daughter in her arms, burying her face in Bella's soft ginger hair. "I'll see how it goes. I plan to use him to get what I want, and if that means telling him we have a daughter, I'll do it."

"He doesn't have a right to know about her."

"Lizzie." Chaz had come up behind his wife and placed a hand on her shoulder. "Let Rikki handle this herself…and let her have some time alone with the baby before she has to leave."

Chaz ushered Mom out of the room and blew Rikki a kiss before shutting the door.

Rikki collapsed in the rocking chair, cuddling Bella in the crook of her arm. As she sang softly to her baby, Rikki let the tears spill onto her cheeks.

She didn't know what she'd do when she came face-to-face with Quinn McBride—the man who'd tried to kill her and had gotten her locked up in a North Korean labor camp.

The man she still loved.

QUINN STUMBLED INTO his apartment and made his way to the kitchen, rubbing his eyes. He banged his shin on the coffee table and scowled at it. "Who put you there?"

He yanked open the fridge door and studied the sparse contents as he swayed on his feet. Giving up, he slammed the door, and the condiment bottles rattled and clinked against the beer bottles.

His stomach growled. The taxi driver had refused to wait for him outside the restaurant where he'd wanted to pick up some food, and Quinn didn't want to get stuck walking home through the streets of New Orleans lugging a bag of food, especially without a weapon at his side.

And he didn't trust himself with a weapon right now—not in his condition.

He fumbled in his back pocket for his cell phone and scrolled through his contacts. If he couldn't get to the food, he'd make the food come to him.

His thumb swept past Rinaldi's Pizza and he

backed up. Rikki's name jumped out at him, grabbing him by the throat. As he hovered over her name, his finger shook, and it had nothing to do with the booze coursing through his veins.

He'd kept her number on his phone and had even called it once or twice just to hear her low, sultry voice caress his ear. But the last time he'd tried to call it, the harsh tones of an automated operator told him the cell number was out of service, and he had no business trying to contact the woman he'd sent to her death.

Dropping his chin to his chest, Quinn smacked the cell phone against his temple. If only he'd shown more restraint out there on the DMZ. He could've taken out both of the soldiers holding Rikki. She would've responded in an instant, would've been able to take appropriate evasive action.

She'd been one of the best damned operatives in the field.

The CIA and navy had clouded his judgment, had accused Rikki of being a double agent, had sent him there to take her out. If he hadn't been so damned eager to please his superiors, he would've gone in with a backup plan.

He always had something to prove.

He wiped the back of his hand across his mouth. He needed to stop playing back the incident in his head over and over every day. Rikki was gone. The CIA was happy. The navy had sent him out on another assignment, which had allowed him to stuff everything away as he'd concentrated on the mission, and now that he was home on leave, he could erase it from his mind another way—the old-fashioned McBride way.

He hunched over the kitchen counter, bringing the phone close to his face. Avoiding Rikki's number, he placed a call to Rinaldi's and ordered an extralarge pizza with everything on it.

When he ended the call, he smacked the phone on the counter and yelled out to the empty apartment, "That calls for another beer."

His stomach rumbled again as he stared at the fridge, and suddenly the effort required to grab a bottle and twist off the top overwhelmed him. He went into the living room instead and crashed onto the sofa, grabbing the TV remote on his way down.

He clicked through the channels, settling on a true crime show about some cold-case murder, and stuffed a throw pillow beneath his head.

The doorbell startled him awake, and the remote fell from his fingers, which had been dangling off the sofa. He ran his tongue around his parched mouth and swept his wallet from the coffee table.

He peered out the peephole at the pimply-faced kid on his doorstep and swung open the door.

The delivery guy's eyes popped open as he held out the pizza box. "Your pizza, sir."

God, he must look even worse than he felt. He handed the kid more money than he should've just to compensate for scaring the hell out of him.

When he collapsed back down on the sofa, Quinn rewound the show, since he'd dozed off during most of it—*dozing off* being a polite term for passing out stinking drunk.

Before digging into the pizza, he retrieved a bottle of water from the fridge and downed half of it before making it back to the sofa. Three slices later and no closer to figuring out whodunit, Quinn closed his eyes and tipped his head back against the sofa cushion.

This time, the click of a gun near his temple woke him up.

Other than blinking once, Quinn didn't move one muscle. Then he spread his hands in front of him and said, "Take what you want, man. Wallet's on the table. Anything you can carry out is yours."

The gunman behind him huffed out a breath and then purred in the low, husky voice that haunted his dreams, "You sure have gotten soft since trying to kill me, McBride."

Chapter Two

Quinn jerked forward and cranked his head around. He choked as he stared at Rikki—but not Rikki—behind the Glock. She always did prefer a Glock.

Her blue eyes had been replaced by a pair of dark brown ones, narrowed in rage. Long, straight strands of brown hair framed her face instead of the thick, wavy red locks that used to dance on her shoulders like tongues of flame, tickling his body when they made love.

"Rikki?" He held out a trembling hand and then clenched it, cursing his drunken state. Maybe this was all an alcohol-infused hallucination. "Is it really you?"

She stepped back, wrinkling her nose. "You smell like a brewery."

Then it hit him. Her presence two feet away sobered him up like a cold shower and a pot of coffee, and his blood hummed through his veins with elation. "How are you here? I—we thought you were dead."

She took another step back, her aim at his head never faltering. "Yeah, too bad for you the North

Koreans wanted me more alive than dead. That shot the soldier took grazed me, nothing fatal, but at least it protected me from the bullet waiting up on that hill—a bullet from a deadly navy SEAL sniper."

"I wasn't going to do it. Why do you think I took out the other soldier? I realized you hadn't turned traitor the minute I saw you make a grab for your guard's gun. I couldn't get a clean shot at the soldier holding you, but I thought you might be able to take care of him yourself."

Her lashes dipped over her eyes once. Her mouth softened, and for a crazy minute he almost took that as a sign to kiss her. *Yeah, if he wanted a bullet between the eyes.*

"That's a good story. At what point during your prep for the assignment did you realize the CIA *spy* you were supposed to eliminate was your former lover?"

"Not right away."

"But even if you had known immediately, you never would've turned down the mission, would you?"

He lifted a shoulder. "I received an order. The CIA had proof."

His words, spoken aloud now to Rikki's face, sounded tinny and paltry to his own ears. How would they sound to hers?

She snorted. "And of course you would've had to reveal that you'd carried on a fling with a CIA operative while we were both on assignment in the Middle East."

"If I had doubted the evidence against you in any way, not only would I have owned up to our…affair, but I would've tried to convince them to call off the hit."

"Instead you charged right in like the good little soldier you are, all honor and duty." Her dark gaze flickered to the half-empty pizza box and the two bottles of beer on their sides at the base of the coffee table.

"All I needed to see was one shred of proof contradicting the CIA's story—and you gave it to me when you charged that soldier. That's why I shot the other one. I was trying to give you a chance."

"Are you sure you didn't kill him because you were afraid I'd already passed along secrets to him?"

"They were low-level grunts marching you along the DMZ. I didn't figure that was the time and place you were going to spill intel. Besides—" Quinn kicked the pizza box out of the way and braced his foot on the edge of the coffee table "—if I'd wanted to take everyone out, including you, I would've started with you first and then dealt with the two soldiers."

She flipped back her dark hair with a shrug of her shoulder. "Maybe."

"I had you in my crosshairs, Rikki. Had you there for a while. I could've dropped you at any time. I couldn't do it."

The corner of her eye twitched. "What does the CIA think? I know my name's not cleared, so whatever you told them, it didn't have much of an impact. Unless you told them nothing and took credit for eliminating a CIA spy."

He scratched his unshaven jaw. How did she know her name hadn't been cleared? How did she get out of North Korea? "I told the CIA and my commanding officers in the navy exactly what happened. Told them their intel must've been wrong, that the North Koreans had you as a captive."

"They didn't believe you?"

"They didn't care. I also told them the North Korean soldier had shot you dead. Case closed."

"Except it's not closed, is it? Here I am."

At least the gun had slipped a little from her grip. Even in his current muddled state, he probably could disarm her. Then again, nobody ever benefited from mistaking Rikki Taylor for an easy target.

"How'd you get out of North Korea? How'd you get here? Where have you been the past—" he counted on his fingers "—sixteen months? And can you get that gun out of my face?"

"If I do, will you take me down? Call the CIA and turn me in?"

He rubbed his eyes and pinched the bridge of his nose. "Do I look like I'm in any condition to do that?"

She cocked her head. "You do look pretty bad, but I'm not stupid enough to underestimate a navy SEAL sniper—even one I shared a bed with. Or maybe that should be *especially* one I shared my bed with."

"Ouch." He held his hands in front of him, wrists

pinned together. "You can tie me up or cuff me if you want."

A light sparked in her eyes, and her nostrils flared, the heat between them still palpable.

Desire and need surged through his body, making him hard.

"Drop your pants." She waved the gun.

He swallowed. He'd been kidding, but he should've known better than to kid with Rikki—not in her current frame of mind. "You're serious?"

"Damn right. I can't check you for weapons, but at least if you're naked I can make sure you're unarmed."

"Rikki..."

"The last time we were together, if you want to call it that, you had me in the crosshairs of your sniper rifle ready to take me out." She steadied her Glock. "What's changed since then except I had the good fortune to escape from the labor camp?"

A knot twisted in his gut. He knew those North Korean labor camps, and the thought of Rikki confined to one of them made him sick.

"Drop 'em."

"Okay, okay." He pushed himself to his feet, feeling completely sober. He unbuttoned the fly on his shorts and yanked them down. The flip-flops he'd been wearing earlier were wedged beneath the coffee table, so the shorts dropped to his bare feet.

"Kick them off and stand away from the sofa where I can see you."

He rolled his eyes but complied, stepping out of

his shorts and kicking them across the room. He could get into a tussle with her right now, but she did have the upper hand.

He stepped away from the sofa and the table and held his arms out to the side. "Nothing on me."

Except the raging erection she could clearly see bulging in his black briefs.

Rikki's gaze dropped from his face to his crotch, and her cheeks flushed. "Now the T-shirt."

Patting his chest, he said, "Do you really believe I have a holster on underneath this shirt? A knife strapped to my back?"

"I'm not taking any chances. Off."

He grabbed the hem of his T-shirt and peeled it off his body. He dropped it to the floor. "Happy?"

"Turn around."

Turning around for her inspection only made him harder. Maybe that would be enough to prove to Rikki that he was on her side—would always be on her side.

When he faced her again, he shoved his thumbs in the waistband of his briefs. "You want the rest off?"

"Don't be ridiculous." She reached behind her back and pulled out a pair of open handcuffs, dangling them from her fingers.

Quinn's mouth dropped open. "No way."

"I know you. I know who you are and what you're capable of. I've come this far, and I'm not taking any chances." She jingled the cuffs. "If you want any more information out of me, hold out your arm— your right arm."

He stretched his arm in front of him. Two more inches and he could touch her soft cheek, tell her everything he'd thought about this past year.

She snapped the cuff around his wrist and yanked on it, the metal cutting into his flesh. "Over here, by the radiator."

He would've preferred the bedroom, but he followed in her wake as she pulled him toward the window.

"Sit down and link the other cuff around this pipe."

He slid to the floor and hooked himself up to the pipe on the radiator. He crouched on his haunches.

Rikki let out a long sigh and placed her weapon on the counter that separated the kitchen from the living room. She dragged a stool from the kitchen and straddled it. "That's better."

"Rikki, I'd never hurt you."

"You were singing a different tune sixteen months ago."

"I explained all that to you. Now that I'm—" he rattled his cuffs against the pipe "—contained, are you going to tell me what happened? What were you doing in North Korea?"

"You mind if I have a beer? Scratch the request. What are you going to do about it?" She hopped off the stool, and he watched the sway of her hips in those tight jeans as she walked around the counter into the kitchen.

Before Rikki sat back down, she tipped the neck of the beer bottle at him. "You keep drinking like you were tonight, and you're gonna trade one six-pack for another...and wind up just like your old man."

He clenched his stomach muscles. She'd been checking him out despite all the tough talk. "North Korea?"

"My partner, David Dawson, got intel that Vlad was meeting with the North Koreans."

Quinn raised his eyebrows. "Vlad?"

"I knew that would get your attention." She took a sip of beer. "David had a way into the country across the DMZ and tagged me to go with him."

"Under the radar of the CIA. They didn't know why you were there."

"David didn't trust anyone, and it turns out he was right." Rikki sniffled and wiped the hand holding the beer bottle across her nose.

"The CIA didn't kill David. They thought you had a hand in his death."

"I know, but they were wrong. The North Koreans killed David and captured me. I had already been their...guest for several days before you spotted me marching along."

"They killed David and were sending you to a labor camp." Quinn bumped his manacled hands against his forehead. "If I had been faster, had taken out the soldier holding you first, you might've had a chance."

"I had no chance, not there. I figured I was a dead woman when I went for the soldier's gun anyway. The area was crawling with North Koreans. You saw that after you took your shot." She dragged her fingernail down the bottle's damp label, ripping a line through it. "I-I thought the person out there was trying to save me and I didn't even know it was you—not until later. And then I found out it was you and you were trying to assassinate me."

He clanged the bracelets against the radiator. "Not when I killed that soldier. I'd changed my mind already. I was trying to help you, Rikki, but I failed, and I've been punishing myself ever since."

Her gaze swept over his unkempt apartment, his tousled hair, the stubble on his face. "Maybe the navy punished you for failing in your duty, for failing to take out the rogue CIA operative."

"They didn't. They figured you were dead and one way or the other, I was the cause of your death." Closing his eyes, he lowered his backside to the floor and drew his knees to his chest. "I'd figured the same thing."

"That's why neither the CIA nor the navy can know I'm still alive." She pinged her fingernail against the bottle. "Not until I can sort all of this out."

"How did you escape from the labor camp?"

"The kindness of strangers."

"The kindness of strangers and a will to survive. I know you, too, Rikki."

"I had a lot to live for."

"Because you got information on Vlad?"

"Yeah, Vlad." Her eyelashes fluttered. "And now I'm going to bring him down and clear my name."

"I'll help you."

She chugged some beer, eyeing him over the bottle. "How do I know I can trust you? How do I know you're not going to run back to your commanding officers and tell them I'm still alive?"

Quinn lifted his hands. "Do you really think I couldn't get out of these if I wanted?"

She sputtered and slammed her bottle on the counter. "Try it."

"I don't want to." He hunched his shoulders. "That's the point. I want you to feel secure. I'm no threat to you, Rikki. I wanna help you."

Someone banged on the front door, and Rikki jumped from the stool, grabbing her weapon. "Who'd you call?"

"Nobody."

"Quinn? Quinn, buddy? You alive in there?"

Rikki took three steps toward the radiator, raising her brows and her gun in his direction.

Quinn whispered, "It's just a friend, an acquaintance from the bar."

Leaning over him, Rikki pushed open the window. As she clambered onto the sill above him, she said over her shoulder, "Get rid of him."

"You're crazy." Quinn tried to grab her ankle with his manacled hand, but she slipped out the window and onto the ledge outside the building.

"Quinn? I know you're in there, buddy. You left your hat at the bar."

A knock followed his words, and a woman's voice came through the door. "C'mon, sugar. Open up, and we can continue the party."

His hat. Damn it. He didn't care about the hat.

Alice's singsong voice continued. "Little pig, little pig, let me in, or I'll huff and puff and blow."

The doorknob rattled, and Quinn's stomach sank when the door started to ease open. He'd forgotten to lock it. He rose from the floor and stuck his head out the window. "Rikki. Give me those keys."

In response, she slid the window half-closed and left him to his fate.

Chapter Three

Rikki heard the door bang open all the way, and the woman with the Southern accent let out a whoop.

"Whatcha doin' there, sugar?"

The man, who seemed a bit more sober, said, "This isn't a burglary or anything, is it?"

Quinn rattled the handcuffs. "Just a little…fun that got out of hand."

The man swore and chuckled. "Is the little lady still here?"

Rikki held her breath as she pressed the palms of her hands against the rough siding of Quinn's apartment building.

"Long gone. Can I get some help here, Elvin?"

"I don't know about that, sugar. I like what I'm seein'."

Rikki didn't blame Ms. Southern Belle. She'd liked what she'd seen of Quinn, too. His slide into despair over her supposed death couldn't have been that dire, given the condition of his hard body. Hard all over. Hard for her.

Elvin grunted. "Alice, if you think I'm going to

hang around while you torture Quinn here, you've been drinkin' too many Hurricanes."

"Who said anything about torture, and who said anything about you hanging around?" Alice must've walked toward Quinn, as her words carried right out the gap in the window.

Rikki shuffled a few steps on the ledge to the left.

"I finally got Quinn right where I want him, as soon as he loses that underwear."

Quinn cleared his throat. "Yeah, well, I think I've had enough fun and games for the night. Thanks anyway, Alice."

Elvin interrupted Alice's foreplay. "Do you have the keys, man?"

Rikki traced the outline of the cuff keys in her front pocket. At least Elvin seemed to be in a hurry to get out of there. A nearly naked man in handcuffs would probably give this good ol' boy nightmares.

The handcuffs jangled against the radiator. "She took the keys. Must've thought it was pretty funny."

"You want me to call a locksmith or something? Go home and get my saw?"

"God, no."

Quinn practically shouted, and Rikki couldn't help the smile that curved her lips. Served him right for leaving her for dead in the DMZ.

"Grab a paper clip from the drawer by the dishwasher. There should be a bunch of loose ones in there. That'll do it."

Rikki heard heavy footsteps and then heavy breathing near the open window.

Alice asked in a low, hoarse voice, "You sure you don't wanna give me a whirl, sugar? I know I could do you better than the girl who left you here."

"No offense, Alice, but I'm not sure you could. She wore me out."

Rikki clapped a hand over the laugh bubbling on her lips and teetered forward.

Finally, Elvin came to the rescue. "Will this work?"

"That'll do it. Right there."

A scrape and a click later and Quinn said, "That's better. Thanks, man, and thanks for picking up my hat. I could've lived without it."

"We'll get out of here. Maybe that little firebrand will return."

Quinn raised his voice. "I hope so."

"Can we at least take the pizza?"

Quinn answered, "Go for it, Alice. I'll see you guys around."

"Maybe another time, sugar, when you're not so... tired."

Quinn mumbled something incoherent, and Rikki closed her eyes and took a deep breath, thankful she didn't have to listen to some other woman having her way with a naked and chained-up Quinn.

The front door shut, and Rikki's eyelids flew open. Now Quinn was free, probably armed and most likely pissed off.

The window beside her slid open the rest of the way, and Quinn stuck his head out. "Are you okay out here? God, I had visions of you tumbling off my building."

Rikki tossed her head. "It's a wide ledge and it's so humid out here, I'm practically stuck to the side of the apartment."

"Come here." He stretched out his arms. "And for God's sake, be careful."

She sidled along the wall and ignored his help when she got to the window. "I got this."

When Quinn stepped back, Rikki swung into the room, her gun in the waistband of her jeans. She drank him in, still in his briefs, a light sheen of sweat dampening his chest.

"Why did you do that? Why'd you leave me hooked up to the radiator?"

"How was I supposed to know your front door was unlocked? If I'd known that, I wouldn't have gone through all the trouble of breaking into your place through your bathroom window."

"You left me exposed to that…man-eater." He hooked a finger around one bracelet of the cuffs and dangled them in the air. "I should've taken her up on her offer and left you out on that ledge until morning."

"Why didn't you?"

Her question wiped the smile from his face. "Because you're here, standing in front of me, fulfilling every one of my wishes over the past year, and now I don't ever want to let you go."

Before she had a chance to blink, Quinn had her

in his arms, and hers curled around his neck in a traitorous response.

His head dipped, and his mouth sought hers. The kiss he pressed against her lips tasted like booze and…desperation. Her muscles tensed. She wasn't here to be Quinn McBride's salvation.

The desire that pumped through her veins and clouded her brain began to lift. As if waking from a dream, she planted her hands against the flat, smooth planes of muscle shifting across his chest. She pulled away from his demanding mouth, backed away from the prodding erection that promised a night of heaven and a morass of hell.

"Quinn. We're not doing this." And how much of "this" was a trick to lure her into trusting him?

Quinn's large frame shuddered. He dropped his hands from her shoulders and clenched his fists at his sides.

Rikki felt the loss of his touch like a cold wave washing over her. Tears ached in her throat. While she'd been locked up, she found out it had been Quinn behind that sniper rifle, and her hatred of him had kept her alive in the labor camp—that and his baby in her belly.

Without her anger, what did she have left but love? And loving Quinn McBride had only ever brought her heartache. That's all love ever brought.

Flexing his fingers, he turned away from her and plucked his shorts from the floor. He stepped into them and ran a hand through his messy hair. "I just hope you believe me, that I'd changed my mind about the assignment. You can't stand there and tell me that if the CIA had given you orders to take me down, you wouldn't have done it."

"I guess we'll never know." She shoved her hands in her front pockets to stop herself from reaching for him again and smoothing her palms against the muscles that bulged and dipped beneath his flesh. "It's not like we were…together at the time of your mission, anyway."

He sliced a hand through the air. "Don't put that on me. I tried to follow up with you, but you'd disappeared and wouldn't respond to my messages."

"I had my own assignment going on. That's when David told me about Vlad and the North Koreans. At the end of our affair, I thought we'd decided to call it what it was."

"And what was it, Rikki?" He crossed his arms over his broad chest, the skin across his biceps tight.

She flipped the unfamiliar dark hair over her shoulder. "A fling—a dangerous, ill-conceived fling that defied all the rules of the navy and the CIA. A fling that would've gotten both of us written up and reprimanded."

"You really believe that shooting you offered me a way out, a way to keep our affair secret?" His dark eyes narrowed to dangerous slits. "What we did wasn't the brightest move on either of our parts, but it wasn't enough to get me court-martialed or ruin my career. And you spooks break the rules all the time to justify the means in the end."

Licking her lips, she took a step back. "I've never slept with someone to get intel."

"Neither have I."

"I didn't mean…" She waved one arm over his shirtless body. "I didn't think that's what you were doing here."

"Really? 'Cause you sure pulled away fast. The Rikki I knew wouldn't have been able to turn off her desire like that. The Rikki I knew ran as hot as blazes."

A pulse beat at the base of her throat, and tingles ran up the insides of her thighs. Their need for each other had been undeniable and unquenchable. Whenever he'd touched her, she'd responded like a feral creature, her hunger not satisfied until he'd taken control of her body and mind in every way, slaked her thirst, tamed her wild cravings. He'd been the only man in her life who'd understood what she needed—before she'd understood it herself.

Her nipples crinkled under her T-shirt, and the familiar wanting throbbed between her legs. Beneath half-closed lids, her gaze wandered to the handcuffs Quinn had let slide to the floor.

If he didn't ask now, if he didn't wait for her consent, if he restrained and ravished her body like he used to, he'd fill the need she'd carried with her since the day she left him in Dubai.

She cleared her throat and stuck out her hand. "Truce? You don't get in my way, and I won't kill you."

He ignored her outstretched hand. "I can help you.

corner. A green neon sign announced the Gator Lounge, and Rikki surveyed the pedestrians behind her before ducking inside the darkness.

She shivered as the air-conditioning hit her warm skin. She'd overdressed for the heat and humidity in jeans, a blouse and tennies, but shorts and a T wouldn't have worked for breaking into Quinn's place and carrying a weapon and cuffs.

Her gaze flickered across the small cocktail tables and then rested on the back of a man seated at the bar, a blue baseball cap on his head.

Rikki scooped in a breath and threaded her way through the tables. As she hopped onto the stool next to her contact, she waved at the bartender.

"What can I getcha?" The bartender slapped a napkin on the bar in front of her.

"Light beer, no glass." She slid a glance to her right to see if her words registered with the man in the Dodgers hat.

She waited for his prearranged response—a folding of all four corners of his napkin.

He picked at the label on his beer bottle with his fingernail.

She held her breath.

The bartender placed her beer on the napkin. "Three dollars. Running a tab?"

"No." Her eyes glued to her contact's cocktail napkin, she unzipped the front compartment of her purse and pulled out a five.

Finally the man beside her dipped his head. "I have what you want, but who are you?"

The question had her convulsively clenching her fist around the bill in her hand. That was not part of the deal. He wasn't supposed to ask any questions. He was supposed to hand over a flash drive with information—after folding the damned corners of his napkin.

She turned toward him and smiled sweetly. "You can't possibly have what I want...sugar. And who the hell are you?"

He jerked his thumb upward, hitting the bill of his cap.

Rikki's heart stuttered. None of this made sense. He had half of the plan right, and it couldn't be just a co-incidence. Who else would be wearing a Dodgers cap in this particular bar in New Orleans at this exact time?

Her laugh tinkled as she creased her money and tucked it beneath a candle. "Sorry, I'm no Dodgers fan. In fact, I don't even like baseball."

Wedging one foot on the floor, she took a quick gulp of her beer. She needed to abandon this rendezvous—and fast.

As she shoved herself to her feet, the man grabbed her wrist and growled in her ear, "I have a gun pointed at your ribs. Make a move, and I'll take you down."

Chapter Four

Quinn plowed through the crowd of people on Bourbon Street, stepping on a few toes and upsetting a few drinks. The Gator Lounge occupied a side street, and he made for the corner of that street like a heat-seeking missile.

Before he stepped through the front door of the bar, he tugged his baseball cap low on his forehead. If Rikki made him as soon as he walked into the bar, he'd lose his chance to find out what business she had in New Orleans. He might lose his chance of ever seeing her again.

Shoving his hands in his pockets, he hunched his shoulders and dipped his head. Two steps into the bar, he scanned it quickly, and his heart jumped in his chest.

His gaze locked onto Rikki and a man in a blue cap heading for the back of the bar. Quinn had frequented enough bars in the past few months to know this one led to an alley running behind it. Rikki and her companion were headed either for the restrooms or out the back door. Either way, he'd be in the vicinity to intercept them.

He backed out of the Gator Lounge and jogged through a small courtyard between buildings. He hugged the side of the bar and poked his head around the corner into the alley.

The blood in his veins ran cold as he watched the man propel Rikki in front of him—by force. Every line in her body screamed that she didn't want to be in his company or be going anywhere with him.

Plenty of people had seeped into this alley off the main street, and Quinn joined their ranks, edging closer to Rikki and her abductor.

The guy in the cap seemed distracted. He didn't notice the pedestrians who passed by him and Rikki, wasn't expecting any kind of intervention—and that was the way Quinn liked it.

Quinn joined a trio of late-night revelers and as they walked past Rikki and the man, Quinn dropped back. He reached out and grabbed the man's arm, twisting it behind him before he could use the weapon gripped in his hand.

Rikki made a muffled cry and dropped to the ground.

Quinn gave the man's arm a quick yank and heard the crack of his bone.

The man howled, his legs buckling beneath him.

Quinn heard a shout behind him. "Hey, hey. What are you doing?"

Plucking the gun from the man's useless arm, Quinn kicked him in the gut for good measure.

Someone came up behind Quinn and grabbed his arm. "What are you doing?"

As Quinn shrugged off the stranger's hand, he slid the man's weapon beneath his shirt. "Dude was taking off with my girl. You're comin' home with me, Lila."

Rikki grabbed the sleeve of Quinn's T-shirt, glanced over her shoulder at the concerned onlooker and shrugged. "Jealousy."

Quinn hustled Rikki out of the alley before someone called the cops or an ambulance. When they hit Bourbon Street, Quinn whipped the hat from his head and clasped it against his side with his arm. "Are you okay?"

"I'm fine. How the hell did you know where I was?"

"Car?"

"Scooter a few blocks away."

"You wear a helmet with that thing?"

She poked him in the side. "You're concerned about helmet safety at a time like this?"

"Let's get that helmet from your scooter, and then we'll hop on my bike."

"If you see me to my scooter, I'll be fine."

"Oh, no, you don't." He gripped her upper arm. "I'm not letting you out of my sight. Some guy with a gun almost took you away—again. I wanna know what kind of danger you're in, and I wanna help. I owe you that."

"Really…" She tripped as he pinched her arm tighter. "Okay. My scooter's around the next corner."

Quinn loosened his hold on her and smoothed his fingers over the bunched material of her blouse. If he'd learned anything about Rikki during their short affair, he knew she didn't respond to halfhearted attempts at persuasion—or lovemaking.

She pointed to a small electric job with a white helmet locked to the back. "That's it."

"Let's grab it and go. You don't know if they ID'd your vehicle or followed you."

"No." She bent over the scooter and released her helmet. "I was not followed from your place— unless it was by you. How'd you know where I was?"

"Later. My motorcycle is back toward the bar." He patted his waistband. "I got the guy's gun, so unless he has a backup he's not going to be taking any shots at you."

"The way his bone cracked when you twisted his arm behind his back, I don't think he could handle any weapon right now." She crossed her arms over her helmet, hugging it to her midsection.

"When I saw him hustling you away at gunpoint, I wanted to do worse than break his arm, but I don't need to be charged with murder or even questioned at this point. Who was he?" He placed his hand at the small of her back and propelled her across the street.

"Later."

As they reached the other side of the street, Quinn ran his hand along the waistband of Rikki's jeans, sitting low on the curve of her hips.

She stiffened beneath his touch. "I don't think it's the time or place to be groping me."

"I'm not groping you, unless you want me to." He briefly cupped her derriere through the tight denim. "What happened to your gun and handcuffs?"

"He relieved me of them and dropped them in a Dumpster right outside the club."

Quinn muttered an expletive. "Maybe we can retrieve them tomorrow."

"We?"

"Here's my bike. Get that helmet on and hop on the back."

She placed a hand on his shoulder. "Are you okay to drive this thing? You were sleeping off a bender when I sneaked into your apartment."

"The events since that time have gone a long way to sober me up."

She held out her hand. "Doesn't matter how you feel, Quinn. Your blood alcohol level is probably still over the legal limit. You don't want to get arrested for murder *or* driving while under the influence."

He jingled the keys and glanced down at his Honda. "Can you manage a bike this size? It's not your little scooter."

She snorted. "Hop on the back."

Rikki handled the bike like she handled everything else—with confidence and ease. He did have to help her hoist the bike onto its kickstand, but she'd been right about taking the wheel—or the handlebars. He'd been an idiot to take a chance like that on the bike, no matter how sober he felt, but he couldn't stand to see her waltz right out of his life just after he'd discovered she'd survived the ordeal in North Korea.

How the hell had she escaped that torture?

As they approached his front door, Rikki hung back. "You didn't leave your place unlocked again, did you? We're not going to find Alice waiting in your bed, are we? Or worse?"

"I can dispense with Alice easily enough, but if that man who had you at gunpoint has any friends, we want to make sure he hasn't ID'd me and dispatched one of his cohorts to wait for us."

Rikki's brown eyes widened as if the thought had never occurred to her. If it hadn't, her spy skills needed some refreshment.

Where had she been since escaping from North Korea?

He tucked her behind him. "Wait here while I give it a quick check."

Her hand grabbed his side, and she lifted her abductor's gun from his waistband. "Now I'm armed, too. We'll take 'em on together."

"I forgot who I was dealing with." He unlocked his door and pushed it open slowly with his foot. When it stood wide, he entered his apartment with his weapon sweeping the room.

Rikki closed and locked the door behind them and crept in beside him, peeling off to check out the back rooms. She called out, "All clear."

Quinn peered over the counter into the kitchen. "All clear here."

Rikki joined him and blew out a breath. "How

would that guy have ID'd you? He barely got a look at you before you took him down."

"If he knows who you are, he might make the connection from New Orleans to me and me to you."

"There aren't many people who knew what we did in Dubai." Her lashes fluttered, and she got busy putting away the spare gun. "I mean, that we...hooked up. I don't think some random person from intelligence is going to make that link between me and you."

"Intelligence? Is that who that was? You said it yourself earlier. The CIA thinks you're dead."

She raised her shoulders to her ears. "I don't know who he was, and more important, he didn't know who I was."

"Are you telling me that was some kind of random abduction?" Quinn shook his head. "No common street thug is going to get over on you, Rikki, especially when you have a gun and cuffs on you."

"I didn't say he was a common criminal. The guy had mad skills himself and I'm not downplaying your heroic rescue, but he'd let his guard down by the time he got me outside the Gator Lounge. He wasn't expecting anyone to come riding to my defense."

"You think he was from the Company?"

"I don't know. We didn't get that far in our acquaintance, but he did not know who I was. He asked me."

"Maybe I am still drunk." Quinn massaged his temple with two fingers. "If he didn't know who you were and he was some kind of spy, why was he abducting you and why were you meeting him?"

Rikki hopped on a stool, straddling it, knees wide. "First, you. How did you know I was going to the Gator Lounge when I left here?"

"I didn't know you were going straight there when you took off, but I saw the text message come through." He clicked his tongue. "Careless, Rikki. I was looking straight down at your phone, but then maybe you wanted me to see that message."

She shot up on the stool, her back ramrod straight. "That's ridiculous."

"Now you. Who were you meeting at the Gator and why?" He held up one finger. "And don't even try lying to me."

She slumped, her shoulders rounding, her hands on her knees. "I don't know exactly who I was meeting. We had a series of clues for each other, a back-and-forth, starting with his Dodgers cap."

"That guy was wearing a Dodgers cap. What happened?"

"I spotted him at the bar, everything on track. I ordered a beer, using the agreed-upon language, but he didn't reciprocate. He went off script. My contact didn't know who I was and wasn't supposed to ask, but this guy…" She waved one hand in the air.

"You figured he wasn't your guy or maybe your guy had been replaced? What did you do?"

"I admitted nothing to him and was getting ready to abandon the mission. I must've telegraphed that because the next thing I knew, he had his gun poking me in the side."

Quinn crossed his arms, curling his fingers into his biceps. "Did he ask you any more questions at that point?"

"Nope. Started marching me away to God-knows-where." She captured the unfamiliar brown hair in one hand and curled it around her fist.

Quinn's gaze locked onto the dark, silky strands. Even without her wavy red hair and bright blue eyes, he'd recognized Rikki in a flash. Why wouldn't he? She'd been in his dreams nightly.

He tugged on a lock of his own hair, which he'd grown out since his previous deployment. "Is that a wig? It's so…different."

Her mouth formed an *O* and released a little puff of air. "I thought we were talking about my abductor."

"We are, we will, just wondering about the transformation." The warmth from his chest began creeping up his neck.

Even discussing a violent incident and a mystery, Quinn couldn't tamp down his attraction to Rikki. He could take her right now, across that kitchen counter, bent over that stool, and not give another thought to her mysterious meeting or the man he'd beaten down in the alley.

What did any of it matter with this woman back in his life, sitting right in front of him, inches away?

She tossed her head, and the dark hair flowed over one shoulder. "It's not a wig. I had my hair straightened when I had it colored. It'll last for several weeks—as long as I need."

Quinn ran both hands over his face as if waking from a long, drugged sleep. "As long as you need to do what, Rikki? What are you doing in New Orleans? What was that meeting all about?"

"The man I was supposed to meet had something for me, something that might help me clear my name. I need that. I need something before I can go to the CIA and reveal that I'm still alive—and no traitor." She blinked and rubbed her nose with the back of her hand.

The Rikki he knew, the woman who'd dumped him in Dubai, never cried. But that woman had been a trusted CIA operative at the top of her game and still on the rise.

When she'd succumbed to him, knowing her superiors would frown on her conduct, knowing she could be reprimanded, she'd spun out of control. Their desire for each other had been so great they'd both thrown caution to the wind. They'd made love in glass elevators high above the glittering city, coupled in the warm waters of the Persian Gulf in a place that frowned upon spouses holding hands in public.

And during all of it, the kick-ass CIA operative who could disarm a man without breaking a sweat and interrogate a suspected terrorist for twenty-four hours straight had relinquished control to him in every way. She'd waited for his commands, done his bidding, which was really her own. She could pretend to herself that he'd mastered her mind and body, but in reality he'd been the captive. She'd enthralled him. Still did.

Quinn launched forward and crouched beside her. His thumb swept her bottom lashes where a single teardrop trembled, although she'd willed it not to fall.

"You deserve that life back, and I'm going to help you reclaim it. What did your contact have for you?"

"A-a flash drive containing some information. I don't think he even knew what the info meant, but he was going to pass it along to me."

"On whose authority? Who's your contact at the agency? Who sent him?"

Rikki swept her tongue along her bottom lip. "Maybe it was all a setup. Maybe the goal of the plan all along included my capture. The flash drive a ruse to lure me out."

"Who sent him? Not some anonymous source? You didn't trust some anonymous CIA drone, did you?"

"It was Ariel." She hunched forward, her nose almost touching his. "You know Ariel, don't you?"

"The head of the Vlad task force. Several of my SEAL team members have been on assignments controlled by Ariel—and they trust her, or him."

"Her. Ariel is definitely female."

"How do you know that? I think one of my team members actually spoke to her, but we're not even sure it was the real Ariel." Quinn's eyes narrowed. "You know her?"

"Ariel was my mentor at the CIA when I started.

You know, one female spy to another in a department dominated by men."

Quinn sat back on his heels. "You mean, you know the *real* Ariel? The actual woman behind the clever pseudonym? From what I understand, the Vlad task force is controlled by Prospero, Jack Coburn's black ops organization. Ariel, Prospero—from the Shakespeare play."

"Yeah, I remember my Shakespeare and yeah, Ariel is with Prospero now, recruited from the CIA several years ago."

"Her real name?"

Rikki ran her fingertip along the seam of her lips. "Ariel."

Quinn jumped to his feet and paced in front of the window. "You don't owe her anything if she set you up."

"I can't be sure she did. She's the one who discovered I was in the labor camp and not dead. She's the one who helped me escape, get back to...get out."

"Maybe she did all that so she could dial in the CIA and have them recapture you. Maybe she didn't want you hobnobbing with the North Koreans, possibly passing them intel."

"I don't believe that, not...Ariel. If that's what she wanted, my contact at the bar would've followed through with our assignment without alarming me, and then she could've sent the FBI to pick me up and arrest me." Rikki slid from the stool and edged around the counter into the kitchen. "That's not how this went down."

"Maybe the contact himself went rogue. Maybe he recognized you."

She made a half turn from the fridge, a bottle of water in her hand. She raised it. "In this getup? Just because you had me figured out immediately doesn't mean some CIA agent is going to recognize me from a photo in a briefing on spies within the Agency. Dark hair, dark eyes…" She patted her hip. "A few extra pounds. This is a damned good disguise."

When she touched her body, Quinn's gaze followed her hand. Rikki had always been long and lean. He tracked up the curve of her hip to the loose blouse draped over her form, brushing the ample swell of her breasts.

He swallowed hard. He'd always enjoyed Rikki's slim, athletic build—especially given their marathon lovemaking sessions in…unusual places and circumstances. But for the first time this crazy evening, he noticed the new softness of her body—the way her jeans hugged her derriere and thighs, the seductive sway of her hips when she walked, the way her blouse pulled tight across her breasts when she spread her arms or gestured. His erection pulsed again.

Then he blinked. Rikki hadn't just escaped from a North Korean labor camp. She'd been recuperating somewhere.

Quinn cleared his throat. "God, it's late. You're bunking here tonight, and I don't want to hear any arguments."

She snapped her mouth closed and chugged some

water from the bottle. "Okay, but just so we're clear you're sleeping in the bed and I'm taking the couch."

Quinn's erection ached for relief, and he tugged on the hem of his cargo shorts. "Yeah, of course, but I have a sofa bed in my office and you can have that." He opened his mouth in a pretend yawn. "We can try to figure out what happened to your contact tomorrow. If you still trust her, get in touch with Ariel."

Rikki sloshed some water in her mouth before swallowing. "Do you happen to have an extra toothbrush?"

"I'm on leave, and you're in luck because I just went to my dentist two weeks ago. I think he's under some misconception that the navy supplies me with one toothbrush every two years, because he loaded me up. They're in the second drawer on the right. This place has two bathrooms, so you're welcome to the other one."

"I'll take the water with me to bed." She swept her small purse from the counter. "This is good. I'll get a good night's sleep and regroup in the morning. I'm sure Ariel will have an explanation for me."

"If you think you can trust her."

"I do." She turned at the entrance to the hallway. "Thanks for your assistance tonight, Quinn. Maybe I *did* want you to see that text after all."

"You can always ask me, Rikki. You can ask me for anything."

A smile trembled on her lips, and then she disappeared down the hallway.

Cocking his head to the side, Quinn listened as

she got a toothbrush from his bathroom and then shut herself in the other one.

He sprinted down the hall and ducked into the second bedroom. He pulled out the sofa bed, darted to his bedroom, snagged a pillow from his bed and tossed it onto the sofa bed. Despite his best efforts at a quick assembly, Rikki hovered at the door of the office as he dragged a blanket across the bed.

"Just making up the sofa bed. Did you find the toothbrush and toothpaste okay?"

"Yep." She ran her tongue along her teeth.

"Okay, then. Tomorrow." His gaze darted to Rikki still propping up the doorjamb. She didn't expect him to squeeze past her, did she? He couldn't handle that.

A few seconds later that seemed like minutes, Rikki pushed herself off the door. "Nice apartment. I had memorized your address from…before. I was hoping you still lived here."

He spread his arms. "Still here. Sleep tight."

He practically ran from the room, slamming the door behind him. Sleep tight? What did that even mean, anyway?

He brushed his own teeth and studied his reflection in the mirror. He needed a shave—and an attitude adjustment. Rikki didn't want him anymore. She'd made that clear before. And after he'd gone on a mission to assassinate her? Yeah, pretty much killed any thread of a chance he had left with her. Now if he could only send that message to his body.

He yanked the covers back from his bed and pulled off his T-shirt. He unzipped the fly on his shorts and hooked his thumbs in the band of his briefs as he started to take them down with his shorts. He usually slept naked, but maybe leaving on his underwear would protect him from lustful thoughts about Rikki.

He crawled between the sheets, rolled on his side, then the other side, and then flopped onto his back, one arm flung across his face. Briefs, no briefs, fully clothed, suit of armor—didn't matter. Rikki Taylor was in his blood, and now she was back in his life.

About an hour later on the edge of another feverish dream, Quinn bolted upright in bed, his heart racing. He paused and heard the noise that had awakened him.

Someone pounded on the door again.

Quinn rolled out of bed and grabbed the gun on his nightstand. He crept toward the front door and paused, holding his breath.

The pounding resumed, following by a groan and a shout. "Quinn? Quinn, you there?"

Quinn drew his brows over his nose and released the locks. He eased open the door, and a man fell across the threshold, bruised and bloody.

"Quinn, you gotta help me. They're gonna kill me."

Chapter Five

With her blouse pulled on over her panties, Rikki tiptoed to the office door, the gun Quinn had taken from her abductor clutched in her hand.

She opened the door a crack and sucked in a breath as the men's voices, Quinn's and someone else's, carried down the hallway.

Had he called someone to take her in?

She rubbed her eyes. If that were the case, the guy wouldn't be banging on the front door in the wee morning hours. She pressed her ear to the gap in the door, wrinkling her nose. She couldn't hear a damned thing.

With the gun leading the way, she edged down the hallway and tripped to a stop.

Quinn looked up from tending to a badly beaten man stretched out on his living room floor. "Put down that gun and soak some towels with water."

The authoritative tone of his voice had her jumping into action. She placed the weapon on the kitchen counter and scurried back to the hallway, where she rummaged through a few shelves, sweeping towels into her arms.

In the kitchen, she ran two of the towels beneath the faucet until they were soaked and dropped next to Quinn attending to the injured man.

As Quinn checked the man's injuries, Rikki dabbed the cuts on his face with the corner of a damp towel. "Who is he?"

"CIA."

Rikki dropped the towel and jerked back. "You called him?"

Quinn spit out between clenched teeth, "I did not. He just showed up on my doorstep like this. I don't know what the hell he's doing here, but he's a friend, and I'm not turning him away."

"O-of course not." Rikki grabbed the towel and continued cleaning the man's facial wounds. "What happened to him?"

"I don't have a clue. He appeared and collapsed."

The man moaned, and Quinn leaned in close. "Jeff, Jeff. What happened?"

Jeff peeled open one puffy eye, caked with blood. "Got the jump on me. Beat me up."

"Who? Street robbery? Do you want me to call the cops?"

"No." Jeff dug his fingers into the flesh of Quinn's arms. "On the job."

Quinn's eyes met Rikki's for a split second, and her heart flip-flopped. The CIA on the job in New Orleans? She couldn't stay here. Couldn't stay with Quinn any longer.

Quinn tugged Jeff's shirt back down over his stomach. "I don't see any weapon wounds."

"No weapons." Jeff closed his eyes. "Unless you count the guy's fists."

"You need some ice." Rikki dabbed the last of the blood from Jeff's face. She gathered the blood-stained towels and wrapped them in a plastic bag. She loaded another plastic bag with ice.

When she returned to the living room, Quinn had helped Jeff onto the sofa. Without the blood smearing his face, Jeff no longer looked half-dead.

Rikki perched on the edge of the coffee table, facing Jeff. She thrust the bag of ice at him. "Here. Can you manage?"

"Yeah, thanks." Jeff grabbed the impromptu ice pack and pressed it against the lump forming around his eye.

Quinn started for the hallway. "I'll get you some ibuprofen and water."

As Quinn walked away, Rikki scooted off the table. "I'll get the water."

She and Quinn returned to Jeff's side at about the same time, and Rikki noticed Quinn had pulled on his shorts. That made two times she'd seen the man almost naked in one night, and she didn't have to use her imagination for the rest. They'd spent two whole days together in his hotel room sans clothing. Answering the door for room service had been the only times either of them had slipped into something to cover their nakedness.

Rikki tucked her hair behind one ear and held out the bottle to Jeff. "Here you go. Feeling better?"

She just hoped to God her disguise would see her through and Jeff wouldn't recognize her, but then nobody in the CIA would be expecting to run into Rikki Taylor—the dead double agent.

"I feel a lot better." Jeff tapped his jaw and winced. "I'm really sorry about intruding here."

Heat prickled Rikki's cheeks. *If only.* "Oh, no, we…"

Quinn shrugged and dragged Rikki against his side with one arm, his hand resting perilously close to the under-curve of her breast, his warm skin soaking through the thin material of her blouse.

In her haste, Rikki had yanked on her top but hadn't bothered with a bra and Quinn seemed to be taking full advantage of that fact.

"Yeah, man, bad timing."

Rikki bit her bottom lip. Definitely taking advantage.

"I'll be out of your way tomorrow morning. If I can just stay the night, I think can get back on track."

"Are you sure you don't need medical care?"

"I could use some, but there's nothing urgent. Nothing that can't wait for tomorrow. I'm really sorry, Quinn."

"Don't worry about it. I'm just glad I was here. Can you tell me what you were doing in New Orleans?"

"Can't do that, man, not even for a badass navy SEAL, and especially not in front of your girl here."

"Me?" Rikki tried to wriggle out of Quinn's grasp, but he wasn't having it.

His fingers curled into the curve of her hip. "She can go into the other room."

Rikki nodded, anxious to escape Quinn's realm where she had zero discipline and even less self-control.

"Sworn to secrecy. You know the drill."

"I do know the drill. I wouldn't tell you about my next mission, either." Quinn jerked his thumb over his shoulder. "I've got a spare room with a sofa bed all made up. I even have a few extra toothbrushes."

Rikki bumped Quinn's hip with her own. "Maybe Jeff would be more comfortable out here."

Jeff tilted his head from side to side, stretching his neck. "Honestly? Stretching out on a bed sounds like a sure cure for me right now."

"Make sure that bed's made up for Jeff, honey." Quinn gave her a little shove from behind, and Rikki clenched her fist at her side. He was milking this situation to the max.

She could raise a fuss in front of this CIA agent, someone who would recognize the name Rikki Taylor immediately, but why tempt fate on this crazy night? "Sure, of course. Why don't you find him a toothbrush and clean towel?"

"I owe you one, McBride, more than one."

Rikki scurried down the hallway and slipped into the office. She smoothed out the covers on the sofa bed and grabbed the rest of her clothes and her purse. Then she crossed the hall to Quinn's bedroom.

As long as he'd invited her into his inner sanctum, she'd make herself at home. She swung open the walk-in closet and dragged a T-shirt off its hanger. Still inside the closet, she pulled the blouse over her head and replaced it with Quinn's T-shirt.

Beneath the T-shirt, she skimmed her hands over her body. Would he be able to tell she'd given birth nine months ago? She cupped her breasts, which still felt heavy although she'd given up breastfeeding a month ago in anticipation of her journey.

Reaching around outside the closet, she flicked off the light. Quinn McBride would not be getting a look at her naked body.

The bedroom door clicked softly as she stepped out of the closet.

Quinn's head jerked up. "Where'd you come from? I thought maybe you'd slipped out onto the ledge again."

She tugged at the hem of the T-shirt. "Thought I'd find some proper sleepwear."

His dark gaze scorched her head to toe, making her feel as if she were standing in front of him without a stitch on instead of in a baggy shirt.

"Sorry about that. Jeff deserved my full hospitality after what he'd been through. I had to offer him that bed."

She wedged a hand on her hip. "You're not sorry. You jumped at the chance to kick me out of that bed and lure me into this one."

A slow smile claimed Quinn's wide mouth. "I saw it as a win-win."

He crossed to the other side of the king-size bed and flipped down the messy covers. "Be my guest."

Rikki folded her arms, grabbing handfuls of the cotton material of the T-shirt, her gaze darting around the room. She leveled a finger at the floor. "You can sleep there for just one night. I'm sure you've slept on harder surfaces than that in your illustrious career as a navy SEAL sniper."

"Not happening." He set his jaw in a hard line. "The bed's big enough for the two of us. You stay on your side, and I'll stay on mine."

She looked him up and down—all six feet three inches of rippling muscle. "This bed is barely big enough for you."

"On my honor—" he drew a cross over his heart "—I'm not gonna lay a finger on you, Rikki. What kind of caveman do you take me for?"

Her eyes flickered across his broad shoulders. *The thoroughly delicious kind.* "Okay, okay. We both need our rest anyway."

Quinn returned to his side of the bed and dropped his shorts.

Holding her breath, she watched him out of the corner of her eye. Those shorts had better be the only piece of clothing he planned to shed. She eased out that captive breath when he slid between the sheets in his briefs.

As she positioned herself at the very edge of her side of the bed, Quinn punched a pillow and said, "At least we know your identity is still safe."

Her eyes flew open. "What do you mean?"

"Rikki."

The mattress dipped and she knew he'd turned toward her. "What? What does that mean, I'm safe?"

"You didn't figure it out?"

"Figure what out?" She rolled onto her back, her head falling to the side.

"Jeff was your contact person."

She hoisted herself up abruptly, banging her head against the soaring headboard. "No."

"Of course he was. Instead of meeting you at the Gator Lounge, he met up with someone who wanted to replace him. The man you saw in the bar, the man who marched you out at gunpoint, is the same man who beat up Jeff and stole his baseball cap."

Rikki covered her face with her hands. *Of course.* How could she be so stupid? Had she really believed two CIA covert ops were going on in New Orleans at the same time?

Motherhood had affected her brain in more ways than one. Or maybe she could chalk it up to the distracting presence of Quinn.

"You see that, right?"

"I-I-I do now. Of course, that's clear. I'm an idiot."

"Don't beat yourself up. You've had a rough night, a rough year." He smoothed his palm up her thigh, froze and then snatched his hand away. "Sorry."

His touch had sent goose bumps racing up her inner thighs. "You're right. I didn't register for Jeff at all except as your late-night booty call."

A laugh rumbled in Quinn's chest. "You say that like it's a bad thing. Look, Jeff doesn't know who he was supposed to meet or why. You were smart to stick to code words and exchanges instead of descriptions."

She wriggled up higher against the pillow. "But where's that flash drive? Do you think he has it on him?"

"Do you really think the guy who beat him up and stole his hat didn't search him? Maybe he didn't want to have the flash drive on him when he met you. Maybe he left it somewhere in case the meeting didn't come off—which it didn't."

"If he takes a shower tomorrow morning, I'm not above searching through his clothes."

"I'll strongly advise him to take a shower."

"Wait." She sat up straight, crossing her legs beneath her, under the covers. "Why did he come here?"

"For help. Jeff and I go way back. He knows I live in New Orleans. He's been to my place a few times. He came to me for help." A muscle ticked in Quinn's jaw. "You don't think I had anything to do with his coming here, do you? I hope we're past that suspicion. If I'd wanted to turn you over to the Agency, I could've done it hours ago."

"We're past that." She grabbed the pillow and slid down again, pulling it beneath her head.

"Good. Get some sleep."

Still on her back, Rikki shifted her gaze to the right, taking in Quinn's large frame, positioned on his side, facing her. He'd pushed the covers down to his waist, although the air-conditioning had cooled the room down to a comfortable temperature.

Her eyes had adjusted to the darkness and she drank in the lines of his body, the hard muscles, even in repose, still etched beneath his smooth flesh.

Before she knew what she was doing, before she could stop herself, her hand shot out and she traced her fingertips around one of his brown nipples.

He sucked in a breath. "You don't want this, remember? Don't tease me, Rikki."

She snatched her hand back and rolled to her side, away from him and his irresistible body. "You're right."

Quinn released a long, shuddering breath.

She had teased him with her light touch, had made him hard. Sighing, she drew her knees to her chest, thrusting out her backside, the heat of Quinn's body inches away. Just inches.

She yawned and wriggled into place, her toes skimming his shin, the hair on his leg tickling her.

"Rikki."

She edged toward him, curling one arm around his waist. "Maybe just once, for old times' sake."

He hissed through his teeth. "You're sure about this?"

She pulled her body closer to his, her front flush against his, and breathed into his ear. "I'm sure."

She edged her fingers between the elastic of his briefs and the flat, hard muscles of his abdomen, dragging her nails along the tip of his erection, barely contained by the thin cotton of his underwear.

He shivered. "I've been imagining that all night, but nothing tops the real thing."

She plunged her hand deeper and cupped him with her palm while stroking his tight flesh with her thumb. Her voice, rough with desire, rasped in his ear. "Take me like only you can."

His erection throbbed in her hand, and she could feel her bones melt and her breasts soften in anticipation of his fiery touch.

Quinn hesitated for just a second until Rikki squeezed him and bit the back of his neck.

In one motion, Quinn rose to his knees and ripped the covers from them both. Towering over her, bulging from the confines of his briefs, he growled, "Take them off."

Tingles rushed through her body at his gruff tone of voice, and she started the game. Leaning forward, she took the band of his briefs between her teeth and dragged them down, over his erection. She continued pulling down his underwear with her mouth, past the flaring muscles of his thighs, down to his knees, buried in the mattress of the bed.

Closing his eyes, he plowed his fingers through her hair. "I can pretend it's the fiery red I love."

"Shh." She pressed the pad of her thumb to his lips.

His fingers dug into her scalp as he urged her down. "Take me in your mouth. Taste me."

She closed her lips around his girth, and he moaned in rhythm as she drew him in and out of her mouth.

He pulled away from her, sitting back on his heels. "It's been too long. I can't last like that."

She caressed his shoulders and kissed the spot right above his left nipple. "Tell me what to do next."

He grabbed a fistful of T-shirt. "You can take this off for starters. Why are you still covered?"

She clutched the edge of the shirt, suddenly shy. Would he notice the differences in her body? Would he know what they meant?

She'd been rail-thin when she escaped from the labor camp, four months pregnant. Undernourished and overworked, she'd feared for the life of her baby. If she'd been captive any more than the two months she'd endured, she would've lost Bella for sure.

Instead, she'd wound up in Jamaica with her mother and Chaz, and Mom had coddled her through the duration of her pregnancy, kept her in bed the first two months, well fed and stationary.

Rikki had put on more than enough weight for her pregnancy, and Bella, although born a few weeks early, had posted a healthy weight and length.

During the pregnancy and after, Rikki's breasts had increased in size and softened, her hips had widened, too, and she presented a much different figure than the taut, tight athlete Quinn had first bedded in Dubai.

Impatient with her reluctance, Quinn dragged the T-shirt from her body and yanked down her panties. "That's much better."

With her bottom lip caught between her teeth,

Rikki watched Quinn study her new body. His eyes darkened to unfathomable depths.

Then he reached out and cupped her breasts. The thrill of his touch shot down to her belly and lower, creating an aching need. She arched her back, thrusting her chest forward.

He juggled her breasts in his hands as if testing their heft. "I like this new development."

He molded her waist with his palms and reached back to stroke her derriere. "And this. When you get your job back with the Agency, you should let them know you wanna lay off the PT because someone likes your new curves."

One side of her mouth crooked into a smile. He approved of her appearance, and more important, he'd dismissed it as the lack of rigorous physical training on her part. Not that she planned to keep Bella a secret from him forever. She just needed to get through this, get her life back, and then she'd tell Quinn everything—no strings attached.

He kissed her mouth. "What are you smiling about?"

"I'm just glad you like the difference."

"You're kidding. I wouldn't think you'd give a damn one way or the other." He eased her back onto the bed and straddled her on his knees. He lowered his body and squeezed her breasts around the tip of his erection. "But just in case you do give a damn and need proof? Here it is, baby."

He skimmed his tip down the length of her body, prodding between her legs.

Her knees fell open, inviting him in, inviting him home.

He stretched out on the bed on his stomach, between her legs, his own hanging off the foot of the bed. He placed his hands against her inner thighs and spread them apart.

Butterflies swirled in her stomach, and her legs shook.

Quinn dragged his scruffy chin over her soft flesh, drawing a gasp from her lips. Then he probed her with the tip of his tongue, searching out all her secret places.

She stretched her arms over her head, crossing them at the wrists, in total supplication and surrender. Raising her hips off the bed, she choked out, "More, please don't stop."

"Oh, I won't stop, my little Buttercup, but you wanted to play this game, didn't you?"

The teasing glint in his eye had her desperate laugh ending on a hiccup. Her job demanded that she be strong, in control, tough as nails, and she'd delivered. When she first met Quinn, he'd joked that she could scare the buttercups off their stems. So when she became soft and vulnerable for him, just for him, he'd started calling her Buttercup. It still made her weak in the knees.

But he hadn't forgotten the game they played, and he began in earnest. He removed his tongue from her throbbing, swollen flesh and nibbled on the insides of her thighs. He touched her everywhere in every way, except for the pleasure spot between her legs.

He set every nerve ending on fire, had her thrashing her head from side to side, digging her fingernails into his buttocks, wrapping her legs around his hips—until she quivered and begged beneath him.

"Please, Quinn. Please. I'm aching."

He sat back, his erection bobbing in front of him, his skin flushed, obviously experiencing the same frustrated, agonizing pleasure she was—but that wasn't their game.

"I need you. Only you. I'm begging you."

He gave her burning nipple one more tweak. "Since you asked so nicely, Buttercup."

He buried his head between her thighs, and two flicks from his tongue sent her over the edge.

Her orgasm roared through her, wringing the strength from every inch of her body, draining her, releasing her from every expectation, every responsibility, the sensations of her body taking over her mind, flooding it with pleasure.

She whimpered beneath him as he plowed into her, his hard desire eager and hungry.

Rikki wrapped her arms and legs around Quinn as he spent himself inside her.

After, he shifted from her body and pulled her back against his front, nuzzling the hollow of her neck. "I'm glad you're among the living. It's like I just had Christmas, my birthday and Mardi Gras all on the same day."

"Me, too." She pressed a hand against her stomach to calm the butterflies. Quinn wasn't the bad guy. He needed to know about Bella, however he felt about having a child.

"Quinn?"

"Mmm?"

"I have something to tell you. I-I hope, well, I hope you'll be happy about it." She paused and swallowed. In a hoarse whisper, she said, "I had a baby—your baby."

She waited several seconds while Quinn's breathing deepened and slowed. Twisting her head over her shoulder, she scooted onto her back.

She sighed as she took in Quinn, sound asleep, still blissfully ignorant that he was a father.

THE FOLLOWING MORNING, Quinn woke her up by holding a mug of coffee beneath her nose. "He's in the shower."

"Who? What?" She rubbed her eyes. "Jeff?"

Quinn nodded, and she nearly upset the coffee as she bounded out of bed.

"Relax. I already searched his clothes, which he left on the bedroom floor. I didn't find a thing."

She tripped to a stop and pulled the T-shirt she'd been clutching to her chest over her head. "Do you think you can devise some story to get him to tell you about the flash drive without revealing who I am? Maybe I can just admit I'm the person he was supposed to meet."

"If you do, that'll connect you to me. He's gonna wonder what our relationship is all about."

She grabbed the edge of her T-shirt and twisted it

into knots with her fingers. "Jeff didn't know why he was meeting me. Didn't know who I was. I'm sure he still thinks Rikki Taylor is dead, if he thinks about her at all. He sure as hell doesn't know you had a fling with Rikki once upon a time." She narrowed her eyes. "Does he?"

"It's getting cold." He held out the mug to her. "And no, Jeff doesn't know anything about my personal life."

"Then let's just tell him I was his intended contact last night." She took the mug from him and curled both hands around it.

"I don't like that idea, Rikki. The lower you keep your profile, the better. What if Jeff talks?"

"Doesn't seem like much of a talker. Pretty tight-lipped if you ask me." She took a sip of the black brew and rolled it in her mouth before swallowing it.

"He's discreet, a good agent, but what if he hears something about us from someone and puts two and two together? You've been doing a good job of keeping under the radar."

"We're going to have to reconnect anyway. I'm not letting that flash drive slip out of my clutches if it's something that can help me. He's going to see me then."

"Not necessarily. You can arrange a drop where you don't meet face-to-face. That'll be easy for you to insist on, since Jeff has already been compromised."

Rikki sank to the foot of the bed. What Quinn

said made a lot of sense. She didn't want to reveal any clues to her identity to anyone.

"You're right. I'll arrange a drop with him." She curled one leg beneath her. "Who do you think ambushed him, us or them?"

"Since he's still alive, I'm betting on one of ours—FBI maybe. They could suspect him of being a double agent. The good news is that they were following Jeff and not you."

"All Jeff needs to do is get Ariel to vouch for him without revealing anything else. She's doing stuff not even the CIA knows about."

"Obviously, if she's helping you. Why is she helping you?"

"Let's just say Ariel is a kindred spirit."

"You mean another woman in a male-dominated field. You mentioned that before."

"Something like that." She pulled the T-shirt away from her body. "I'm going to take a shower."

As she brushed past Quinn, he grabbed a handful of her T-shirt and pulled her toward him. "Any regrets about last night?"

"None at all." She kissed the edge of his chin. "You?"

"No, except that I feel like I kinda tricked you, I mean by inviting Jeff to take the extra room."

She snorted. "You didn't have me fooled for one minute, Quinn McBride."

Showered and dressed in the jeans and blouse from last night, Rikki joined the men in the kitchen with her empty coffee cup.

Jeff raised a piece of toast in her direction. "I was just telling Quinn how sorry I am that I barged in on you two."

Rikki squinted at Jeff's black eye and puffy jaw. "I'm glad Quinn was home. Do you need to see a doctor?"

"I might need some stitches." He brushed aside the lock of hair drooping over a bandage on his forehead. "But I'm okay."

Hopping up on a stool at the kitchen counter, Rikki placed her cell phone in front of her. "Then we don't mind at all, do we, Quinn?"

"Happy to help, bro." Quinn held up the coffeepot. "Refills?"

Rikki shoved her cup across the counter, and Jeff nodded as he pulled his cell phone from his pocket.

"Do you want something else to eat, Jeff?" He pointed to the fridge. "Eggs?"

"Nothing fancy. Toast is okay."

Her phone buzzed on the counter, and Rikki grabbed it. Jeff had sent her a text.

Slowly she raised her gaze to meet his. Understanding and acknowledgment flashed between them.

She'd been outed.

Chapter Six

A charged silence descended on the kitchen. Rikki held her breath as Quinn looked up from pulling slices of bread from a bag. His gaze darted from Jeff to her, understanding dawning in his eyes.

Rikki locked eyes with Jeff, his color high. Her chest rose and fell with each breath, her fight-or-flight instinct in high gear.

Jeff ventured first, turning his cell phone outward. "You're my contact, aren't you?"

She ignored the question. "What happened to you last night? You can tell me."

Jeff shifted his gaze to Quinn, his head down, busy with a bag of bread, whistling like an idiot—as if she and Jeff didn't know he was listening to every word they said.

Rikki waved her hand in Quinn's direction. "You can trust him."

Jeff tipped his head at Quinn. "Are you involved in this?"

"Who, me? I'm just making toast." Quinn held up two pieces of bread.

"Quinn's not involved." Rikki circled the edge of her coffee cup with the tip of her finger. "I know him, knew he lived here. Just like you, I went to him for help after things fell apart last night."

Jeff dropped his shoulders as if dropping his guard. "I'm glad to see you're okay. I didn't know what happened after that guy attacked me and took my cap. He was trying to get info out of me, but a cop came by and he took off. He knew where we were meeting but none of the details."

"That became obvious pretty quickly, since he didn't have the sequence of codes down."

"I'm sorry. I would've stayed around to warn you, but the cops wanted to question me. I had to get out of there, and then I passed out in a churchyard." Jeff traced the lump beneath his eye. "He didn't get anything out of you? Didn't hurt you?"

"I-I was able to get away, and that's when I called this guy." She leveled a finger at Quinn.

Quinn shrugged and snatched the toast from the toaster. "I guess I'm the go-to guy in New Orleans."

Rikki crossed her arms on the counter and leaned forward. "Do you have it?"

"Not on me." Jeff patted his pockets. "Thank God. That man would've snatched it in a second."

Quinn slid a plate in front of Rikki. "Do you have any idea who he was, Jeff? Was he one of yours?"

"CIA coming after one of its own? Maybe."

"Let's face it." Rikki pinged her cup with her fingernail. "You were not on official CIA business.

You were on Ariel's business, and she flies under the CIA radar. Maybe someone at the Company picked up your actions and figured you for a double agent."

Jeff leaned against the kitchen counter for support. "I hope not. I don't want to have to do any explaining. After that whole Rikki Taylor thing with North Korea, our agency is on high alert."

Rikki's eye twitched and she rubbed it. "Rikki Taylor is dead."

"Yeah, but not forgotten." Jeff wiped his mouth with the back of his hand and then dumped his coffee into the sink.

She wanted to ask Jeff the meaning of those words but didn't want to show too much interest in Rikki Taylor. Quinn had been right. He wasn't one to kiss and tell, and Jeff didn't know of the connection between her and Quinn.

Now this second chance had fallen into her lap, and she had no intention of letting it slip by.

"Where is it?" Rikki had broken up her toast into several pieces but hadn't taken one bite yet.

Jeff narrowed his eyes. "Why didn't you tell me who you were last night when I staggered across Quinn's threshold? You must've made me right away as your contact."

"Quinn's a friend. I didn't want to expose him— not to you, not to the CIA. He's on leave trying to relax. Just because we both chose to drag him into our business doesn't give us the right to put a target on his back."

"Hey, what are friends for?" Quinn raised one hand.

Jeff nodded. "I get it. I wouldn't have come here if I thought I could get back to my hotel safely."

Rikki's heart flip-flopped. "Nobody followed you here, right?"

"I was careful."

Rikki pressed her lips together. Not that careful if he'd been found out before. "Anyway, I didn't want to pull Quinn into this and didn't want you linking me to him. I figured I could get you to drop the flash drive for me somewhere, and I'd pick it up and be on my way. Less exposure for you, too—you don't know who you met, what she looked like or why you were dropping the flash drive."

Jeff coughed. "I didn't even know it was a flash drive. All I have is a small padded envelope."

"My bad." She exchanged a quick glance with Quinn, who was pretending to clean up the kitchen. Rikki should've known Ariel would keep things as anonymous as possible. "So, can you get it for me now?"

"I'll do you one better. I'll give you the same information I meant to give you at our meeting."

"I'm ready."

"It's in the St. Louis Cemetery Number One."

Rikki's mouth dropped open. "You couldn't leave it in a safe-deposit box?"

"Who's going to suspect a cemetery?" Jeff lifted one shoulder. "It's in the entrance to one of those family mausoleums—the St. Germaines. Two steps down, loose stone six in on the right. Pull that out, and you'll find your flash drive...or whatever."

"Kind of a public place, and it's summertime with lots of tourists. Hope nobody stole it." Quinn crossed his arms, feigning disinterest no more.

"Honestly, I wasn't expecting it to be there overnight." Jeff pushed himself off the counter. "Now I'd like to get out of this city."

Quinn didn't budge from his position, and with his arms crossed and his biceps bulging, he looked large and in charge. "How and where do you think that guy picked up your trail?"

"I don't have a clue." Jeff licked his lips. "Nobody knew I was out here. I was thinking it must've been Ariel. Maybe someone is tracking her communications."

"Why would that be?" Rikki tried to keep the panic from her voice, and she slipped her hands beneath the counter where she twisted her fingers into knots.

"I'm not sure. Have you ever met her?"

Rikki relaxed the lines of her face into a smooth mask. "No."

"Nobody has. Do we even know if she's male or female? Ariel's a pseudonym."

"I'm assuming Ariel is she." Rikki lifted and dropped her shoulders quickly.

"She's a woman."

Rikki held her breath and swiveled her head around toward Quinn. He'd better not out Ariel. Rikki asked, "How do you know that?"

"One of my teammates actually spoke to her. She was going to help him out with an ambush but didn't have to in the end."

"If that's who he was really speaking to. All I know is Ariel is the head of the Vlad task force, and she has a lot leeway, including employing navy SEALs stateside in her efforts to stop him." Jeff wagged his finger at Quinn. "You'd better lie low, or she'll get you, too."

Quinn held up his hands. "I'm trying to, but you never answered my question. Do you know when this guy picked you up?"

"I'm ashamed to say, I don't. He wasn't in a talkative mood while he was punching me in the face."

Quinn stepped aside, clearing the way for Jeff to leave the kitchen. "Take it easy, man, and get those stitches, and, Jeff?"

Jeff glanced down at the hand Quinn had placed on his shoulder. "Yeah?"

"You never came here, never saw me, never saw her here, never saw her period, right?"

"Yeah, yeah. Of course, man." Jeff ducked away from Quinn and nodded once to Rikki. "Good luck."

Rikki let out a long sigh when Jeff closed the door behind him. "What do you think?"

"I don't know." Quinn rubbed his knuckles across the dark stubble on his jaw. "I think Ariel could've picked a better agent to make the drop. Someone obviously followed Jeff from his hotel, from the airport, who knows? And Jeff didn't have a clue."

Rikki slid from the stool and stretched. "At least that guy last night hadn't been following *me*. It seems as if Jeff was the focus of that whole mess. Someone suspects him of double-crossing the Agency. Hopefully, once it's cleared through Ariel, he'll be off the hook."

"Ariel is currently not answerable to anyone in the CIA. I know guys who have been on her assignments. You're lucky she can act at will." He swept her plate with its crumbled toast from the counter and dumped it in the sink. "Why is she looking out for you?"

"I told you. It has to do with Vlad."

"And we know Ariel would move heaven and earth to bring down Vlad. Do you know why?"

Rikki shoved her hands in her pockets. She had no intention of outing Ariel. The woman had her back, and Rikki would do everything in her power to keep Ariel's secrets. "That's a dumb question. Vlad is building a terrorist network across the globe. He's involved in drugs, weapons, assassinations. He's the CIA's public enemy number one. Why *wouldn't* Ariel be hot to bring him down?"

"From what I've heard, it seems…obsessive."

"I don't know. All I can tell you is that David was on Vlad's tail when he proposed that North Korea trip to me."

"Talk about dumb." Quinn slammed his fist into

his palm, and Rikki jumped. "David should never have dragged you along on that assignment."

"Why? Because I'm a girl?" Rikki wedged her hands on her hips.

"No, damn it." In two steps, he ate up the distance between them and grabbed her by the shoulders. "Because I was falling in love with you, and David took you away from me."

Rikki pressed a hand to her chest, above her fluttering heart. "That wasn't going to work, Quinn. It was hot and heavy sex in the heat of Dubai. I left because of my job, a job I couldn't do tangled up in the sheets with you."

He pinched her shoulders, his fingers digging into her flesh. "Don't pretend that's all it was between us. I'll admit, the sex was exciting, crazy—just like last night—but you know there was more than that."

She stroked his wrist. "Your libido can play tricks on you sometimes."

"I'm a man, not a boy." He softened his hold on her, smoothing this thumbs across her clavicles. "I know the difference between sex and love. When you left me—" he thumped a fist against his chest "—I felt it here, not farther south."

"And when you got the assignment to kill me?"

"God, Rikki." He spun away from her. "Didn't we go through this yesterday? I didn't know it was you until it was too late to back out. They'd already convinced me of your guilt before I got the name and picture of my target. If it had been so easy to prove your innocence and call off the hit, where was your precious Ariel? How come she didn't do anything about it?"

"Like you said, the proof was there, but someone manufactured that proof against me and David. That's what I hope to discover from the flash drive— information about who double-crossed us. That's my starting point."

She backed up from the heat emanating from Quinn's body. She wanted to get on safe ground and away from Quinn's feelings. Had he really just mentioned love?

She'd always been afraid of hearing that word from any man. For her mother, it had been a magic spell, and she'd dragged Rikki around from man to man, giving up everything for that one little word. Rikki had a mission, a career, or at least she'd had one. Even if she did clear her name, she had Bella now.

Her stomach sank. She had to tell Quinn about his daughter. If she really did want to push him away, keeping his daughter from him would cement that. She couldn't do that. For all Quinn's sexy manhood, he had a big heart. He'd fallen for her, foolishly and disastrously, and here he was admitting it. Any other man whose lover had left him would never fess up, never make himself vulnerable to that woman again. And yet here he was.

Of course, he'd had a sniper rifle trained on her last year.

He dragged both hands through his hair. "Okay, your starting point is that flash drive. Let's go get it."

"You know where this cemetery is?"

"Of course I do. Every good N'awlins boy does. I'm not sure how we're going to march up there and remove a stone from a mausoleum in the middle of the day with tour groups wandering around."

"I am not going to a New Orleans cemetery at night."

"It's not deserted. There are tours at night, too. Those might be the more popular tours."

Rikki cocked her head. "Should we join one of those? Just two tourists on a cemetery tour at night? We could break off from the group to examine the St. Germaine mausoleum more thoroughly. That way, if anyone tracked Jeff there, we wouldn't stick out."

"You had the same thought I did." He swung his leg over the barstool, straddling it. "How long had Jeff's attacker been following him?"

"That's exactly what I thought. Maybe he hadn't been tailing Jeff closely enough to see him stash something at the cemetery, but he could've seen him go there." Rikki bumped her forehead with the heel of her hand. "I can't believe some of Jeff's actions."

"He would pick a cemetery." Quinn raised one eyebrow. "Sounds like Jeff was watching too many spy films."

"I guess he just never figured he was being followed. This wasn't a regular assignment for him. He probably jumped at the chance to do a favor for Ariel and the Vlad task force."

"Maybe." Quinn strode into the living room and slid his laptop in front of him on the coffee table.

"What are you doing?"

He looked up. "We're gonna book a tour of St. Louis Number One tonight."

THEY'D DECIDED AGAINST the midnight ghost tour. The one after dinner in the dark would be creepy enough.

Rikki had wanted to get the grand tour of New Orleans with Quinn as her guide. She'd been to the city just twice before, but Quinn had a love of his hometown and would've been able to do it justice.

He'd put a stop to that idea, however. Although the chances were low, Quinn didn't want to run into Rikki's attacker from last night. They took a quick trip to Rikki's run-down motel to collect her possessions and check her out of the room, and then reclaimed her scooter from the French Quarter.

Quinn had insisted he could protect her better at his place, and Rikki didn't doubt that, but they both knew they'd wind up in bed together for as many nights as she stayed.

She needed to use one of those opportunities to break the news about Bella. Quinn hadn't wanted children, as his own mother had abandoned him, and his father never let him forget it. Even though Quinn's dad was an alcoholic and the adult Quinn knew his mother had run from him, the child within Quinn never stopped blaming himself. Then he somehow figured if both his father and mother had been uncaring parents, how could he possibly be any better?

Rikki couldn't imagine Quinn as anything but

a loving, doting father. It was one of the things about him that had scared her off—his ability to feel deeply.

She thought she'd been getting into a relationship marked by kinky sex and a shallow appreciation of each other's bodies. But Quinn was right. It had started developing into so much more—and had scared the hell out of her. David's call had come just in time.

Later that night, Quinn emerged from the back rooms with his freshly washed hair slicked back and a towel around his neck. He eyed the sundress she'd changed into when they went to her hotel. "You're not going to change into all black for the occasion?"

"In this heat?" She fanned herself with her hand. "No, thanks. Maybe my floral dress will keep the ghosts at bay."

"Or maybe it will bring them out to force you to have some respect for their final resting place."

She pointed at his light-colored shorts. "I see you're dressing more for the weather than the occasion."

"It's almost July. I'm not crazy."

She combined the remains of their Chinese food into a couple of containers. "Thanks for dinner, but take-out Chinese is not exactly what I was expecting in New Orleans with all the fantastic restaurants here."

"We're not on vacation, despite the tour. We don't know where that guy is or even who he is. He could be lurking around waiting for you."

"Unless Jeff has already reported back to Ariel and gotten the all-clear."

"Nobody told you yet, so you're gonna lie low."

She poked her head around the refrigerator door while putting away the leftovers. "This is your dream come true, isn't it? To keep me captive in your apartment?"

He widened his eyes. "You're making me sound like a perv. I just wanna keep you safe."

"I know that." She slammed the fridge door. "I can't stay hiding out here forever, can I?"

"No. I don't expect that. I meant what I said that first night. I want to help you get your life back—even if that life doesn't include me."

She turned her back on him and dumped their dishes in the sink. That life would have to include him once she told him about Bella.

Thirty minutes later, Rikki climbed onto the back of Quinn's motorcycle and pulled on her helmet. Quinn had a small car he used while in town, but he always used his bike downtown for parking purposes. That was why she'd rented a scooter—she'd needed to get in and around the city quickly.

Quinn claimed a parking spot for his motorcycle at the edge of a small lot about a block from the cemetery.

Rikki slid from the back of the bike as Quinn tipped it to the side. She pulled the helmet from her head and shook out her hair.

"I'll take that." Quinn took her helmet from her and locked it on the back of the motorcycle along with his.

He took her hand, and they jogged across the street toward the rambling cemetery behind a wrought iron fence. He led her to a group of people hanging out by the entrance gates, and they joined the rest of the tourists, taking pictures with their phones and peeking through the gate.

Several minutes later, a tall African-American woman with long braids and a gauzy skirt floated up to the group. "Everyone here for the tour? I'm Aida, your guide. We'll take care of earthly matters first if you'll hand me your printed ticket or show me the ticket on your phone. Then we'll get to the unearthly matters."

One of the tour members, who'd had a few too many Hurricanes to drink, let loose with a ghoulish laugh.

Aida raised her brows at him. "Taunt the spirits at your own risk."

Despite the real ghouls Rikki had encountered over the past year, she sidled up next to Quinn and tucked her hand in the crook of his elbow.

Once Aida had checked all their tickets, she led them into the cemetery and stopped at a small grave site with an ornate cherub guarding it. She rested one hand on the cherub's chubby winged foot. "This is the sad resting place of AnaBella Lafleur. She died at the tender age of five, but her wealthy father forbade her burial in the family mausoleum because he never accepted her as his daughter. He had suspected his wife of cheating on him, and even after the child's death, he never got over it and ended up murdering his wife."

The warmth of the evening couldn't suppress the little chill that ran up Rikki's back. She tugged on Quinn's arm and whispered, "Jeff and his morbid ideas."

As the group moved past AnaBella's grave, Quinn brushed his hand over the headstone. "Poor Bella."

Rikki tripped over a crack, and Quinn steadied her. "Whoa."

She pulled him away from the group. "Once we find the St. Germaines, let's get out of here. I don't want to hear about any more dead children."

He cocked his head at her. "You okay?"

"Nervous."

"I don't blame you. It's gonna be okay."

He draped an arm over her shoulder, and she welcomed the heavy pressure of it. Why had he called that girl Bella? It must have been a sign.

Aida delivered the history and the atmosphere as the group moved from grave site to grave site, and Rikki might've enjoyed this tour another time.

A half hour into the tour, Aida stopped at a Baroque-style mausoleum with heralding angels on either side of the entrance and a profusion of flowers carved in stone and trailing down the columns.

Aida folded her hands in front of her. "This is the St. Germaine mausoleum, notable for its Baroque style and detailed stonework."

As Aida's smooth voice hummed in the background, Rikki elbowed Quinn, her mouth dry. She scooted closer to the steps, and someone asked if they were going inside.

Aida replied, "Not this one. There's a smaller one toward the end of the tour, and a few people at a time can duck inside."

Aida continued talking about the stone carvings as Rikki took one step down, pretending to study the writing on the side of the mausoleum.

The group began to shuffle off, and Rikki took the next step down, running her fingers over the rough stone on the right—six in, loose stone. Aida had better not catch her and Quinn defacing a crypt.

Aida's voice grew fainter, and Quinn joined her on the second step. "Did you find it?"

"Not—" her fingers scrabbled over the stone, looking for a gap or a give "—yet."

She crouched down and flashed the light from her phone on the wall.

Quinn crouched beside her, bumping her shoulder. "Is it loose right here?"

She shoved the heel of her hand against the spot he'd indicated with his middle finger, and the stone seemed to rock.

A scrape and a shuffle had her spinning around, knocking into Quinn as he straightened up, reacting to the noise.

Rikki's throat tightened as she looked up at the drunken man, not looking so drunk now, his face lit from below, his eyes narrowed.

"What are you two doing down here? And why don't you let me in on it?"

Chapter Seven

Quinn instinctively stepped in front of Rikki. "Just doing a little historical investigation."

"Yeah, right." The man pulled a gun from his waistband, a silencer attached to the barrel.

Quinn's own weapon burned against his back, useless. He held up his hands. "Look, man. We don't want any trouble. We were just looking around."

"Looking around for something that spook left you?" The man laughed. "The CIA needs to do a better job of screening its applicants."

Rikki squeaked next to Quinn. "CIA? What are you talking about? I thought you were a cemetery ranger or whatever and thought we were defacing the mausoleum. You really are drunk."

The man glanced quickly to his side as laughter rose from the group. "Who are you?"

Quinn raised his hands higher, hoping Rikki might see the gun stuck in the back of his waistband, beneath his shirt, and hoping she might be able to get her hands on it. "Buddy, we're a couple of tourists on a cemetery tour. I don't know what your game is, but we don't have any money on us and you're not going to get too far with our credit cards."

Another laugh from the group had the man licking his lips and sliding one foot off the top step.

That was all Quinn needed. With the man off balance, Quinn charged him, knocking him backward. The gun tipped up and Quinn made sure it stayed that way by slamming his fist against the man's elbow.

The force and placement of the blow caused the man to drop the gun, and Quinn kicked it away. As the man came at him again, Quinn grabbed him by the throat.

"Now it's your turn. Who the hell are you?"

"Is there a problem?" The tour guide hovered several feet away. "Are you two fighting?"

Under the cover of the shadows, Quinn put the man in a sleeper hold. He slumped, and Quinn lowered him to the ground.

"I think this guy had a little too much to drink. He was bothering us, but no harm done." He jerked his thumb over his shoulder at Rikki, who'd been no help at all. "My wife's done with the tour, though."

Rikki stepped over the prone body and brushed off the skirt of her dress. "Yeah, I've had enough."

Aida put her hand to her heart. "Do I need to call the police?"

"If you want to report a drunk in public." Quinn slipped the tour guide a twenty. "Thanks. Great tour."

Putting his hand at the small of Rikki's back, he

propelled her through the cemetery as if they had a couple of ghosts on their tail.

When they escaped through the gate, Quinn let out a breathy whistle. "How the hell did he pick us up? And what the hell were you doing back there? Didn't you see the gun in my waistband?"

"I saw it, but I was attending to more important business."

"Really? There's more important business than saving my life?"

She plunged her hand into her purse and pulled out a folded envelope. "I got the stone loose and grabbed the envelope Jeff left for me."

He pinched her cheek. "Smart girl, but I guess you answered my question."

"Your question?" She took one skipping step next to him.

"That envelope is more important than my life."

She gave him a shove from behind. "I knew you could handle that guy."

"Thanks for the vote of confidence." He pulled out his weapon. "Still didn't answer the first question, though. How'd that guy make us? He walked up a little later, after we met the group out front."

Rikki took a step back and wrapped her fingers around the bars of the cemetery fence. "There are at least two of them. The drunk in the cemetery and the guy who beat up Jeff and tried to hustle me out of the bar last night."

"There could be more." Quinn dangled his gun at his side as they started down the street. "The good news is that they don't seem to have a clue who you are."

"And they might not be CIA. Sure didn't sound like he worked for the Agency, did it? If they did, wouldn't Jeff had already cleared himself through Ariel? The CIA must know by now that Jeff wasn't involved in any counterespionage. So why would they still be after the flash drive?"

He pulled her close to him. "Let's get home right now. We'll talk about this later. I'm worried that dude in the cemetery has a partner out here."

"We already know what his partner looks like. He tried to kidnap me last night."

"If it's just the two of them."

"Who the hell are they if not CIA? Why were they following Jeff?"

"I think we need to talk to Jeff again."

Quinn didn't let out the breath he'd been holding until they reached his motorcycle. Once on board, Quinn gunned the engine and took a different route back to his place, keeping an eye on his mirror.

They returned to his apartment unnoticed, and Quinn let Rikki off the bike before tucking it into his parking space next to his car.

They walked inside his place, and he fired up his laptop. "Let's see what's on this flash drive, and it better be worth all the trouble."

Rikki dug into her purse, pulling out the envelope. She ripped it open and dumped the flash drive into her palm. "Okay. I'm ready."

She sat next to him on the sofa and scooted in

close as she reached past him to insert the flash drive into the side of his computer.

Quinn double-clicked on the device when it appeared on his display. He ran the cursor down the list of files. "Emails. Is that what you were expecting?"

"I didn't know what to expect. Ariel indicated she'd run across some files that might be useful to me."

Quinn opened the first email, and Rikki gasped beside him.

"They're David's emails."

"To you?" Quinn hunched forward and squinted at the addresses at the top of the message. "No. Who's Frederick Von?"

"I have no clue." Rikki grabbed the laptop with both hands and brought it close to her face, as if that would help her identify the recipient of David's email.

"It sounds like he's discussing his trip to South Korea."

"It does, but that's strange." She placed the computer back on the coffee table. "I thought the two of us, David and I, were the only ones in on that trip."

"He probably had to get approval from someone."

"That someone was Ariel." She tapped the keyboard. "Let's see the next one."

After Rikki opened four emails in a row, Quinn whistled. "Looks like David was two-timing you. He sent all these messages to Freddy, and they all seem to be referencing the trip to South Korea that he took with you."

"Frederick Von." Rikki drummed her fingers on the edge of the laptop. "That name sounds familiar to me."

"Another agent?"

"Not sure." Rikki clicked back through the emails, and then slumped against the sofa. "This doesn't tell me anything. These are mundane messages about a trip I was on. They make no sense to me. Why would Ariel think these would be useful, and why would those men following Jeff go to such great lengths to get them?"

Quinn squeezed Rikki's thigh. "Maybe there's something in the simplicity of the messages. Why would David be relaying insignificant details about his trip to someone—unless the details mean something else?"

She shot up. "Like a code?"

"That makes more sense to me than these emails."

She opened the first email again and read it aloud. "'Frederick, the trip to South Korea is on. We have intel about our man. I'll follow up with time and location.'"

"Time and location for what? Did the two of you meet anyone in South Korea before you crossed over?"

"Just our guide. I'm not sure what happened to him after David was murdered and I was captured."

"I'm assuming your guide wasn't Frederick Von."

"No. His name was Buddy Song."

He bumped her knee with his. "Let me have a look." Jabbing his finger at the next open email, he said,

"This email, which is the next one in the sequence, doesn't have any more information about the promised time and location. This one discusses car rental details."

"We didn't rent a car." She tilted her head to the side and caught her long hair with one hand. "Buddy picked us up and drove us around. This email doesn't even make sense."

"None of them do." He'd clicked open several more and bounced among the messages. "These are in order by date, but the subject matter isn't sequential."

"A code." She tossed her hair over her shoulder. "The emails are significant in another way, a way only Frederick understands."

"How'd you do in secret code class?"

"Secret code class?" She snorted softly. "No such thing."

"Yeah, right. I know you agents learn stuff like that. Hell, we reviewed it ourselves. Were you an A student in deciphering like everything else?"

She sucked in her bottom lip, clamping it between her teeth. "Something like this? It could be anything—position of letters, single words, and the entire message might be run across all the emails with different rules for different messages."

"But there are people at Langley who specialize in this, aren't there?"

Spreading her arms, Rikki kicked her feet up on the coffee table next to the computer. "Do I look like I'm in with Langley? They think I'm dead, and good riddance. Do you think Langley would appreciate learning that Ariel from a black ops organization got into one of their dead agents' emails? That ain't gonna happen, McBride."

He tapped one finger on the laptop. "That's all right. I have my sources, and they're not connected to the Agency."

"Like Jeff? No, thanks."

"I said my source is *not* with the Agency." He put his feet up next to hers and tapped them with the ball of his foot. "Are you giving up? You went through a lot to get this flash drive. Ariel must've understood the significance of finding a set of David's emails, and she went through a lot to get them to you."

"Who said I was giving up?" She draped her leg over his and wiggled her toes against his ankle. "I'll give it a try. I just don't understand why David was sending coded messages to someone about our trip."

"Maybe he had a different reason for taking that trip, one he didn't reveal to you."

Closing her eyes, she tipped her head back against the sofa, but she was anything but relaxed. Her hands curled into fists in her lap, and her eyelids flickered and twitched.

"What is it? He told you he had info about Vlad, right? Maybe that wasn't it at all. Maybe he just said that to get Ariel's support…and funds."

"Yes, he said we were on Vlad's trail, but that's not what I'm thinking of. David was…different on this trip. I thought about it after he died, and figured I was reading too much into his behavior because it was the last assignment we'd do together, but he was definitely in a different place."

"In what way? Do you think he was lying to you? Had he ever lied to you before?"

"Once." She opened one eye. "And it wasn't about work."

"What then?"

"Love."

Quinn raised his eyebrows. "He lied to you about love?"

"Yesss." The word came out like a hiss.

Quinn waited. If Rikki wanted to tell him, she'd tell him. She'd found the perfect profession for her temperament. She kept secrets like nobody else he knew…had kept secrets from him.

Rikki sighed and sat up, drilling him with her gaze so that he clenched the muscles in his stomach and prepared himself.

"David was in love with me…or at least he thought he was."

A muscle flickered at the corner of Quinn's jaw. What man in his right mind *wouldn't* be in love with Rikki? "I thought David Dawson was a married man."

"He is…was. That was the problem, or at least one of them. I told him in no uncertain terms I didn't fool around with married men, and of course I felt guilty that maybe I'd led him on."

"You didn't. You're no tease." Quinn ran a hand over his mouth. "How'd he take it?"

"Not well—at first. He gave me all the old excuses

married guys trot out—Belinda didn't understand him, the marriage was in name only, he thought she might be having an affair of her own, they were on the verge of divorce." She squeezed the back of her neck. "Then I dropped the other shoe."

"Which was?"

"Even if all those things were true, I wasn't in love with him, and I apologized for suggesting otherwise."

"How'd he take *that*?" Quinn didn't even have to imagine David's despair at the news, as he'd felt it himself when he woke up in that empty hotel room in Dubai with a white sheet of paper on the pillow next to him.

"Better than I expected. He didn't rant or rave or protest or even try to convince me I felt differently. Although it pained me, I suggested we work apart for a while, but he wouldn't hear of it. Insisted he could cope and keep our relationship on a purely business level—and that's when he lied to me."

"He kept up his protestations of love?" He could almost feel sorry for the poor sap, but at least Quinn had taken it like a man and never had contact with Rikki again—until it came time to kill her.

"David never mentioned it to me again, but I knew he still had feelings for me." She ran her hand down Quinn's arm and threaded her fingers through his. "I could tell he did when you came onto the scene."

"Me?"

"David knew about us in Dubai, of course. David and I knew each other so well, he could tell. He got all fatherly on me and played the role of the mentor, which of course he was. He warned me about what having a fling while on assignment could do to my career." She pulled his hand to her lips and kissed his knuckles. "As if I could've stopped that wild-fire between us even if I'd wanted to—and I didn't."

"Until the end." He disentangled his fingers from hers so that he could think straight. "Is that what happened? Is that why you left me high and dry? David's sage advice?"

Now he felt no sympathy for the man, but had an itching desire to punch him in the face—except he was dead.

"No." She brushed the hair from his forehead to torture him some more. "I realized our relationship belonged in the short and combustible category."

"You realized that without discussing it with me, then. I could've combusted like that forever."

A low chuckle vibrated in her throat, and he swal-lowed. The damnedest things about her could make him hard.

"Anyway, David's cautionary words didn't have any influence on my leaving you and Dubai."

"Maybe his cautionary words didn't, but his ac-tions did." Quinn sat up on the edge of the sofa, mak-ing a half turn toward Rikki. "If you don't think he pulled you out of Dubai to go on this wild-goose chase in South Korea to separate us, you're naive—and I've never considered you naive before."

"I suppose there was that element to it, but David

was hot for this mission and wanted me along." She shrugged.

Quinn snorted. "David was hot for you. He never did leave his wife, did he? That horrible, half-baked, failing marriage."

"No."

"So, that was the one time David lied to you. Said he'd accepted you two would never be more than colleagues but all the while harboring that fire down below."

She held up her finger. "Careful, you're talking about a dead man and a damned good agent who died for his country."

"You're right." He grabbed her finger and kissed the tip. "If he lied about that, how do you know he wasn't lying to you about other things, like this trip to South Korea?"

"Because he wasn't a very good liar, was he? He couldn't hide his feelings for me."

"A CIA agent who's not a good liar? He should've found another career."

Rikki cocked her head. "I mean, he was a good liar. If you could've seen him in action with our contacts…masterful."

"Then he could've been masterfully lying to you about Korea."

"Not to me." She shook her head, and her dark hair slipped over her shoulder.

Quinn wrapped his finger around one silky lock, missing her red curls. "Overconfident much?"

She bit her lip. "Pretty smug, huh? You're right. He could've totally been playing me, but why?"

"I can't tell you, but it sounds like David used you as a cover and put both of you in danger. Stupid move." Quinn stretched and then pointed to his laptop. "Are you going to look at these anymore?"

"I'm calling it a night." She pushed herself up from the sofa. "At least we have one thing to be grateful for."

He snapped the lid of his laptop closed and stood up next to her, resting a hand on her hip. He was just grateful Rikki was alive and back in his life—sort of. "I know what I'm grateful for."

Her lips formed an *O*, and a blush washed over her cheeks. "I-I meant that those people out there who were following Jeff don't seem to know who I am or what they're looking for."

"Yeah, of course." He pinched her hip. He didn't want to put Rikki on the spot. If she chose to fly away once she found whatever it was she was looking for, he'd let her go.

She'd gutted him the first time she left him, but her supposed death and rebirth had given him perspective. As long as Rikki Taylor was living and breathing in this world, he'd take that as a win.

Twisting his T-shirt between her fingers, Rikki leaned into him and kissed his chin. "Meet you in bed."

"You go ahead and get ready. I'll lock up."

Quinn checked his doors and windows and stopped to stare down at the dark street. Rikki had been right. They hadn't been on anyone's radar until Jeff had been compromised. One of those two men or both had been following Jeff before they even accosted him. They'd tracked him to the cemetery but hadn't been able to see what he'd done there.

The one guy had already ID'd Rikki as Jeff's contact, and the other man must've been keeping watch on that cemetery and spotted Rikki.

But they didn't know who she was, and if they weren't working for the CIA, maybe they didn't care. As far as the Agency knew, Rikki was dead. Did they want to keep her that way?

Quinn twitched the curtains closed and secured his apartment before sailing through the master bedroom to Rikki snug in his bed. "I'm just gonna brush my teeth. Don't steal all the covers before I can make it in there."

She looked up from some papers in her lap. "What is this Quinn, a book?"

He took a detour from his beeline to the bathroom and snatched the papers out of her hand. "Nosy."

"You're writing a book?"

"Nothing definite, just telling some stories—with the names and places changed. Just a collection of ideas at this point. Don't make a big deal out of it."

"It *is* a big deal. You'll have to run it by the navy, won't you?"

"Of course." He waved the papers. "It's in its infancy."

"Had me hooked right away."

He dumped the papers on his nightstand. "Definitely not bedtime reading, especially after the day we had."

Quinn went into the bathroom to brush his teeth and splash some water on his face. When he returned to the bedroom, Rikki had his notes clutched in her hands again, sitting cross-legged on top of the covers.

"Oh, come on. It's not that good."

"I think you've got something here, Quinn. I'd read this."

"Yeah, because you live it." He snatched the papers from her hands again and tossed them on the floor. "I'm looking at something a lot more interesting."

On his knees, he straddled her and buried one hand in her hair, pulling her close.

Her body, usually so pliant and willing beneath his touch, stiffened.

He kissed her mouth, but her soft lips didn't return the kiss. He opened his eyes and ran the pad of his thumb over the crease between her eyebrows. "Too wound up? I can fix that."

"Frederick Von."

"What? David's email recipient? Did you remember who he is?"

"Oh, yeah. I remember now."

Quinn shifted his body and lay on his side, propping up his head with one hand. "Who is he?"

"Frederick Von is a character in David's spy novel."

"That's not what I expected to hear. David wrote a spy novel?"

"He was working on one, and he shared it with me—yours is much better."

"That's a relief to hear, but mine's nonfiction. Why would David be sending emails to a fictional character—his own?"

Rikki crossed her arms and hunched her shoulders. "Frederick Von was the bad guy in David's book."

"I'm not following you, Rikki."

"Frederick Von was the bad guy—a traitor."

Quinn blinked.

"A trai-tor."

Rikki strung out the two syllables as if speaking to someone with a tenuous hold on the English language, and right now he felt as if she *were* speaking in a different tongue.

He shook his head. "You need to give me a break here. One minute I was ready to ravish you, and the next you're staring at me speaking gibberish about some fictional character in a bad spy novel—and it would have to be bad if it's worse than my drivel."

"I think David was being clever for the sake of being clever in those emails, just because he could and nobody would catch on…nobody but me."

"David *is* clever because I still don't understand the significance."

"Von is a traitor, Quinn—just like David."

Chapter Eight

"Whoa, whoa." Quinn held up his hands. "How did you jump to that conclusion?"

"Why the secret emails? Ariel discovered these on a different server, a nonclassified server that wouldn't be under intense scrutiny after his death. There would've been no reason for David to send these emails. The only people who knew about the trip besides David were me and Ariel. David and I communicated in person about the trip. And what do those emails even mean? You said it yourself. They appeared to be cover for a code."

"A code. It doesn't mean David was a traitor just because he used the name of his character, who happens to be a traitor." Quinn slid back under the covers. "If it is true, what do you think David was doing in South Korea if not tracking down a lead on Vlad?"

"I'm not sure, but it all went horribly wrong. David was killed, and I was captured by the North Koreans." She stretched out beside Quinn and rested her head on his shoulder. "The whole assignment was off. I saw the red flags but didn't trust my instincts, like David had always taught me."

"That's convenient. David taught you to go with your gut…until your gut was warning you against him."

"I never thought I'd see the day when I had to look into David Dawson."

"Look into him? How do you propose to do that?"

Draping her arm around Quinn's waist, Rikki nuzzled his neck. "I'm going to pay a visit to Belinda, David's widow."

"That's a dangerous idea. You want to stay anonymous for as long as you can."

"Belinda and I never met. She doesn't have a clue what I look like. She'd know the name, but I'm no longer Rikki Taylor, remember?"

"I think you'd better let me check in on the widow."

"You'd come along?" She fluttered her eyelashes against his face. "You don't even know where I'm going."

"Doesn't matter. If you're going to be doing any investigating, I'm coming with you." He combed his fingers through her hair. "Where *are* we going?"

"I'll have to check for sure, but they lived in Georgia—Savannah. She's from there, so I can't imagine she'd want to leave after David's death."

"We can drive, but I'm not sure what you hope to find out from her."

"It's a start. Besides, most agents confide in their spouses, whether or not they're supposed to. That's why…" She broke off and buried her face in the hollow between Quinn's neck and shoulder. That's why she'd never wanted to get married or have a serious relationship with someone. That's why she'd run out on Quinn without a backward glance. Her career always had to come first. She never wanted to follow in the footsteps of a man.

But now she and Quinn had a child together, and the longer she waited to tell him, the harder it was going to be to spit it out. What was she afraid of? Quinn would welcome the news, despite his own fears of being a bad father.

"Yeah, yeah." He wrapped her in his arms. "That's why you never wanted to get married. We don't have to get married, Rikki, but we can pretend for a few nights."

Then he made love to her in a way that no married man had a right to make love to his wife.

THE FOLLOWING MORNING, Rikki searched for Belinda Dawson and found her in Savannah. She poked at the monitor displaying the address and said, "I think this is a different address from the one she shared with David, but at least she's still in Savannah."

"Then it's on to Georgia today. Map it out and see how far we have to go. It's about a ten-hour drive, if you're up to it. I think it's safer than flying right now, even though you have your fake ID."

"Driving is fine." She entered Belinda's address on the computer. "Will your car make it?"

"It's sturdier than it looks, and I just changed the

oil. Let's get some breakfast, throw a few things in a bag and hit the road."

She tapped the print key and heard the printer in the other room gear up. "That car may be sturdier than it looks, but I know it doesn't have a GPS."

"I'll use my phone's GPS, but we need a plan beyond showing up on her doorstep, especially if you're not going to out yourself."

"We have ten hours to think up a plan." Rikki hopped off the stool and circled into the kitchen. "Besides, we need to get out of New Orleans. You just disabled those two guys. You didn't eliminate them."

"Yeah, can you imagine me explaining two dead bodies in my hometown?"

"At least those two dead bodies aren't ours." She grabbed the coffeepot and raised it. "Eggs or pancakes?"

Two hours later, Quinn aimed his little junker car across the Pontchartrain bridge and they headed out of New Orleans.

Rikki dozed while Quinn drove the first few hours, and she woke up trying to hold on to the last wisps of dreams about Bella. Her heart ached, and she wanted nothing more than to call Mom in Jamaica and hear her daughter's coos and babbles.

She slid a sidelong glance at Quinn. He'd probably want to hear his daughter, too. She had to tell him, sooner rather than later. If she waited for the perfect time, she'd never tell him. There would never be a perfect time to tell him that she'd discovered her pregnancy while on assignment in South Korea and had spent the next few months of that pregnancy locked up in a North Korean labor camp, and then believing the father of her child had tried to assassinate her. Yeah, never a perfect time for that.

"Everything okay?"

"Sure, why?"

"You sighed like you meant it. Are you having second thoughts?"

"About this trip?" *About telling him about his child?* "No. I know this is the right thing to do."

He cocked an eyebrow while drilling the road ahead with his gaze. "The right thing to do? You make it sound like a moral decision. It's just a chance we're taking that Belinda knows something about David's activities before his death."

"I know that." She covered his hand clenching the steering wheel with her own. "It's nice being on the road with you. Do you want me to drive for a while?"

"I can go for another few hours. Then we'll stop for gas, get something to eat, and you can take the wheel."

"Just let me know." She stretched her arms to the roof of the car and wiggled her fingers. "A big guy like you needs a bigger car than this."

"Not the best for long trips, but when I'm home I don't drive it much. I stick with my bike."

"How much more leave do you have?"

"Less than a month, and I intend to help you wrap this up before my next deployment."

"I appreciate it, but that's not why I contacted you."

"I know." He turned up the air. "You looked me up to find out if I was really going to kill you. How did you find out it was me behind that sniper rifle?"

"Not telling." She clapped a hand over her mouth.

"Ariel. It had to be Ariel. What can you tell me about her? Are you close to her?"

With her hand still over her mouth, Rikki shook her head.

Quinn puffed out a breath. "Whatever. I know you female spies stick together. She's risking a lot by keeping your secret and giving you classified information."

"David's emails aren't classified, and Ariel doesn't work for the CIA. She's Prospero and doesn't report to anyone."

"Yeah, Jack Coburn's black ops agency, but I didn't realize she had such free reign."

"Oops, then I guess I did reveal something about her. See how that works?" She snapped her fingers. "That's why we're paying a visit to David's widow."

"About that, now that you've had a nap, let's brainstorm. Who are we and why are we there?"

Rikki drummed her fingers on the dashboard. "We're with the Agency. If she tried to check up on our story, she won't be surprised if the CIA denies our existence. She and David had been married for twenty years. She knows the drill."

"Okay, we're with the Agency. How about from human resources? We're following up on some benefits? Or we're collecting some equipment."

"The second scenario is more likely, since HR

would just call or send an email. If we were checking up on equipment, that would explain our in-person visit."

Quinn skimmed his hands over the steering wheel, warming to the task. "Maybe someone already confirmed that she had David's equipment for pickup. The fact that she doesn't know what we're talking about can be written off as bureaucratic red tape."

"Plenty of that, and your story might give us an excuse to look around."

He let out a short laugh and hit the steering wheel with the palm of his hand. "Would you let two goons from the CIA search your place?"

"After what they did to me?" She rolled her eyes. "I wouldn't let them set foot on my porch."

Quinn took a swig from the bottle of water in the cup holder. "I thought that was the point of this whole exercise. I thought you wanted back in at the Agency."

"I want my life back, my reputation. I want to be able to return to the States as Rikki Taylor without getting taken down at gunpoint."

"And you wouldn't go back to the CIA if they'd have you? Does that mean you're done with the spy business?"

"I don't know." She flicked the air vent away from her and rubbed the goose bumps from her arms.

They'd veered onto dangerous ground here. She didn't want to talk to Quinn about the future—hers, theirs. Right now she just wanted to clear her name and be with Bella without worry. And Quinn? She'd never wanted him more, but she had to tell him about Bella.

"Kids?"

She choked on the water she'd just sipped. "What?"

"Kids. Do David and Belinda have children?"

"They don't."

"Good. I mean, that makes things a little easier, and it makes sense."

"Does it?"

"Why would someone in David's line of work…or yours…want children? Just a complication."

Rikki stuffed her hands beneath her thighs. From the frying pan to the fire. "People do."

"Selfish people."

She reached forward and twisted the knob for the air. "It's cold in here. So, we're CIA paper pushers looking for government equipment. I'm going to use a different name from the one on my current ID. No need for anyone to link up April Thompson from Canada with a CIA agent. Who are you?"

"I'll think about it, but we'll probably need some badges in case she asks for ID."

"You're right." She pressed her fist against her forehead. "I'm sure David taught her to be cautious."

"Do you think you could have someone re-create that badge?"

"To pass someone's brief glance? Sure. Do you know Savannah? I don't. Where would we get these badges?"

"You know as well as I do, there are people in every

city across the country who provide these services—for a price."

She patted her purse, thinking about Baily in Jamaica. "I sure do, but we're not going to have much time."

"Since you can't exactly call one of your former contacts, I can ask one of my teammates to look up something in Savannah for us."

"Your navy SEAL teammates? Would they know?"

"You'd be surprised what they know about covert operations, especially now. Your BFF, Ariel, has been dragging them in from deployment to do her bidding."

"Really?" Rikki folded her arms across her stomach. Had Ariel had an ulterior motive in directing her to stop in on Quinn when she arrived stateside? She hadn't needed much encouragement, as she'd wanted to square things with Quinn first…and tell him about Bella, but Ariel had initiated the idea.

"Why is Ariel using your sniper teammates for these assignments?"

"Because of Vlad. Because we know him. Because he knows us."

She whipped her head to the side. "Vlad knows you?"

"Who do you think nicknamed him Vlad?" He jabbed a thumb against his chest. "That was us, or more specifically I think it was my teammate Alexei Ivanov, the moody Russian."

"Why Vlad? He's not Russian, is he?"

"We don't know what he is. He's a man of many disguises. Just when we think we know what he looks like, he appears as someone else."

"So if he's not Russian, that you know of, why'd Alexei start calling him Vlad?"

"Because of his Russian sniper rifle—the Dragunov. Alexei uses the same rifle. Vlad was a sniper for the opposition forces, any opposition forces, before he started amassing his terrorist network. We came up against him many times. Sometimes we bested him, sometimes he bested us, but we never killed each other. Make no mistake about it, Vlad knows my entire team. I think he even reached out to the Russian mobster who killed Alexei's father just for that reason."

A chill claimed her body, and she'd turned off the air conditioner ten miles ago. "That's scary."

"Yeah, it's personal, so Ariel fights fire with fire. She's involved us in the battle to bring him down. I think I'm the only one who's escaped—and here I am."

"Yeah, here you are." Rikki nibbled on the end of her finger.

Quinn glanced her way and flexed his fingers on the steering wheel "What are you saying? Are you telling me it wasn't your idea to look me up?"

"It was my idea, but…"

"But Ariel was on board." Quinn twisted his head to the side and pinned her with a questioning gaze. "Ariel knows about us?"

Rikki dipped her chin to her chest. "She does.

Sh-she knew before, before I even went on that assignment in Korea with David."

Quinn whistled. "I wonder if she knew you were my target before I did."

"I don't know why she would." Rikki traced the pattern on her skirt with her fingertip. "She's not CIA. Why would the Agency give Prospero a heads-up on their…assassinations? Especially of one of their own."

"C'mon. Prospero has ways of discovering things, even about other intelligence agencies. They're the best in the business."

He picked up his bottle and swirled the water inside.

"I can't believe Ariel knew about our relationship and knew about your assignment and did nothing to warn you."

"She did." Quinn slammed the bottle back in the cup holder. "She did, damn it."

"What are you talking about?"

"After the navy revealed my target to me, along with the evidence of your betrayal, I was sick. I didn't think I could go through with it."

"But the evidence was irrefutable." She twirled her finger in the air. "I believe you."

"When I was already in South Korea preparing for the assignment, I received an anonymous text on my secure phone. Just two words—*she's innocent*."

Rikki gasped and smacked her hand against her chest. "Ariel?"

"Who else? Of course, the text sent me into a tailspin, planted doubts in my head. I couldn't call off the mission based on an anonymous text. It could've been from the enemy. But it was enough. When I saw those soldiers marching you along, guns at your back, and saw your last, desperate attempt to get away from the very people you were supposed to be conspiring with, I knew the truth."

"You're here because Ariel wanted you here with me—looking into who set me up, looking into Vlad."

"Since it wasn't your own idea to contact me, I'm grateful to Ariel for intervening." His lips twisted into a bitter smile.

"She didn't have to do much convincing, Quinn. I wanted to see you. After the initial shock and anger and much reflection, I knew you'd changed your mind about that mission, about me." She rubbed her hand down his bare thigh.

"Where did you do all this reflecting? You haven't even told me where you were after the escape from North Korea."

She owed him. "Jamaica."

"Jamaica?" His thigh muscles tensed beneath her touch. "What's there?"

"My mother and stepfather."

"Ah, the former hippie, right?"

"They've been there for years. My stepfather runs the rental shop out of one of the resorts there—snorkeling equipment, skimboards, parasails. My mother met him there and stayed, which is no surprise. She'd follow any man anywhere, always did."

"I'm assuming the Agency knows about them?"

"Of course, but the CIA thinks I'm dead. No reason to question my mom. I felt safe there."

"If Ariel knew about us, knew you were alive and knew I hadn't gone through with the assassination, why didn't she tell me about you?" Quinn clenched his hands on the wheel, his knuckles turning white.

"She didn't know if she could trust you, Quinn. I didn't know if I could trust you." She ran her fingers over the ridges of his knuckles. "Someone had been actively working against me, planting false evidence. I didn't know how much of that you believed."

"I suppose I don't have room to complain. I *was* stationed on that hillside, ready to take you out." He rolled his shoulders. "I wish it had been someone else."

"I don't."

"You're happy a former lover had you in his crosshairs?"

"If it had been anyone else, I'd be dead."

Chapter Nine

When they reached the outskirts of Montgomery, Quinn eased off the gas pedal. "Keep an eye out for a gas station and a few fast-food joints."

Rikki jerked her thumb over her shoulder. "I saw a sign back there listing a bunch of places. Should be right off the highway, convenient for travelers."

"We're making good time and should be in Savannah before eleven o'clock if we keep moving."

She eyed him up and down, and he felt the familiar ache under her gaze, even after five hours of driving, cramped in the same position. His attraction to Rikki knew no bounds.

"Are you sure you don't need to get out and walk around? We can wait for a rest stop."

"I'm used to hunching in the same position for long periods of time. Doesn't bother me."

"I'm still taking the wheel. You can nap, if you like. Your phone's GPS has gotten us this far, so I'm sure I'll be okay."

"I can sleep anytime, anywhere, even standing up."

"Like a horse." She rapped one knuckle on the window. "Two miles until services."

Two miles later, Quinn took an exit toward a clump of gas stations and restaurants. "Do you have a preference for food?"

"Chicken."

"I think we'll be able to find chicken in Georgia." He made a hard right turn into a gas station. "Let's fill up first. Bathroom?"

"I'd rather wait and use the restroom in one of the restaurants. I don't trust these gas station restrooms."

Quinn filled the tank while Rikki walked around the car with a squeegee, washing splattered bugs from the windows.

"Ugh, these bugs in the south are supersize."

"That's right. You've never spent much time down here, have you?"

"Back in Dubai, you promised to show me around New Orleans sometime." She dropped the squeegee in the soapy water and grabbed a couple of paper towels.

"What do you mean? I showed you a good time on Bourbon Street and we had a helluva cemetery tour."

She bunched the paper towels into a ball and threw it at his head. "You've got a sick sense of humor, McBride."

The nozzle clicked, and he pulled it from the gas tank. "Let's get you some chicken and get back on the road."

Rikki opted for a crispy chicken sandwich so she could eat and drive at the same time.

Quinn lowered the back of his seat and stretched his legs as far as they would go. He grabbed a sweat-shirt from the backseat and bunched it between his head and the window. "I'm gonna catch a few hours of shut-eye if you think you'll be okay. You're going to head toward Atlanta and then veer east."

"Don't worry. I'm good at directions, especially when the nice computer lady spits them out."

"I trust you. You made it out of North Korea." Quinn adjusted his seat again and closed his eyes. At least he trusted her to get them to Savannah in one piece, but he didn't quite trust her to leave his heart in one piece.

Rikki woke him up twice along the way to pull into a rest area to use the bathroom. After the second time, he stayed awake for their arrival into Savan-nah. He pointed out a small motel outside the historic district where Belinda Dawson had a house. "Looks like there's a vacancy here."

"We should pay cash."

"Nobody's tracking me. I'm on leave, and I can do what I damn well please."

"But you're here under an assumed name, which you haven't chosen, by the way. What if Belinda checks you out?"

"You really think she's going to ask us where we're staying and call to confirm our names?"

"Humor me." She jerked her head toward her purse in the backseat. "I have enough cash in there to cover it."

"I'll humor you, and I've got it."

If the motel clerk thought it was strange that they paid for two nights up front with cash, her bored face didn't show it.

When they got to the room, Quinn picked up a card on the desk. "Free Wi-Fi. Can you get on my laptop and re-create a CIA badge? That'll make it easier when we ask someone to produce a badge for us."

"Did you hear from your friends yet?"

He held up his phone. "Two suggestions from two different sources. It's gonna mean a trip to one of the seedier areas of Savannah."

"That kind of stuff always does."

"Yeah, you should know, Ms. Thompson."

"I'm going to use a different name for this identity." Her gaze tracked to the digital clock on the bedside table. "Not tonight?"

"We'll save it for tomorrow. Do you know if Belinda works?"

"She did. I don't know about now, since David's death."

"Nine-to-five job?"

"She's in marketing, and I think she went into an office. So we should pay her a visit at the end of the workday."

"Exactly, but not too late. We don't want to scare her by showing up on her doorstep in the dead of night."

"Poor woman has had enough to deal with. I almost feel guilty nosing around."

Quinn threw himself across the bed and toed off

Dear Reader,

IT'S A FACT: if you answer 4 quick questions, we'll send you 4 FREE REWARDS!

I'm not kidding you. As a leading publisher of women's fiction, we value your opinions... and your time. That's why we are prepared to **reward** you handsomely for completing our mini-survey. In fact, we have 4 Free Rewards for you, including 2 free books and 2 free gifts.

As you may have guessed, that's why our mini-survey is called **"4 for 4".** Answer 4 questions and get 4 Free Rewards. It's that simple!

Thank you for participating in our survey,

Pam Powers

To get your 4 FREE REWARDS:
Complete the survey below and return the insert today to receive 2 FREE BOOKS and 2 FREE GIFTS guaranteed!

"4 for 4" MINI-SURVEY

1 Is reading one of your favorite hobbies?
☐ YES ☐ NO

2 Do you prefer to read instead of watch TV?
☐ YES ☐ NO

3 Do you read newspapers and magazines?
☐ YES ☐ NO

4 Do you enjoy trying new book series with FREE BOOKS?
☐ YES ☐ NO

YES! I have completed the above Mini-Survey. Please send me my 4 FREE REWARDS (worth over $20 retail). I understand that I am under no obligation to buy anything, as explained on the back of this card.

☐ I prefer the regular-print edition
182/382 HDL GMYH

☐ I prefer the larger-print edition
199/399 HDL GMYH

FIRST NAME	LAST NAME

ADDRESS

APT.#	CITY

STATE/PROV.	ZIP/POSTAL CODE

BUSINESS REPLY MAIL

FIRST-CLASS MAIL   PERMIT NO. 717   BUFFALO, NY

POSTAGE WILL BE PAID BY ADDRESSEE

READER SERVICE
PO BOX 1341
BUFFALO NY 14240-8571

NO POSTAGE
NECESSARY
IF MAILED
IN THE
UNITED STATES

his shoes. "We're just there to look around and assess. We're not gonna accuse her husband of anything, but if we see anything that needs closer examination, I'm not gonna rule out making a return visit—while she's not there."

"I agree." Rikki yawned. "I'm tired."

He patted the bed. "Come on over here and I'll give you a massage."

"I know how your massages end." She put her hands on her curvy hips. "I said I was tired."

"I missed you, Rikki. I missed us, but I think I can control myself if you're too tired for sex. Hell, I'm just happy holding you in my arms." And as insincere as that sounded, he'd meant it. "Go brush your teeth and do whatever it is you do to get so beautiful and then I'll deliver a no-strings-attached massage to your aching body."

"Sounds like heaven."

When she returned to the bedroom, an above-the-knee cotton nightgown floating around her body, Quinn turned off the TV and jumped from the bed. "Stretch out. I'll brush my teeth and be right back."

While in the bathroom, Quinn washed his hands with warm water and plucked a little bottle of lotion from the counter. Squeezing the lotion into his hands, he walked back into the bedroom and winked at Rikki. "I was afraid you'd be sound asleep."

"Close to it, but I'm curious to witness this self-control of yours as I've never seen it."

"That's cold." He perched on the edge of the bed,

rubbing his hands together. "No massage oils, but I found some lotion."

"That'll work." She stretched like a cat, pointing her toes off the foot of the bed.

"Um." He tugged at the hem of her nightgown. "Do you want to remove this?"

She twisted around. "I knew it."

"Come on. Even massage therapists who are complete strangers have you disrobe for a massage."

As she pulled the nightgown over her head, she said in a muffled voice, "But they usually have a towel or sheet for the naughty bits."

"Do you really want me to cover you with a towel?"

She tossed the nightgown over her shoulder, and he made a concerted effort to keep his gaze off her luscious breasts.

"Nope. Have your way with me, McBride. You always do." She lay back down on her stomach, her arms at her sides.

He started with her shoulders, digging his thumbs into the sides of her neck.

She let out a long breath of air between her teeth in a hiss. "That feels good."

"Did you forget about these magic fingers?"

"I remember the magic fingers. I just don't remember them plowing into the sore muscles of my neck."

"Shh. You talk too much."

She wasn't kidding about those sore muscles. He worked at the tight knots at the base of her neck until they disappeared, and then he squeezed her shoulders and pressed the heels of his hands into her shoulder blades.

Rikki's breathing had deepened, and Quinn continued massaging the smooth flesh of her back. He expected another sarcastic comment from her when he reached her buttocks, but she moaned softly as he kneaded her glutes.

Her new womanly shape enticed him as much as her fit, athletic build had, but he knew now his attraction to Rikki ran more than skin deep. He'd known it all along, from the moment he met her at that hotel bar in Dubai. He'd known it the minute he awakened in that same hotel all alone.

His loss had punched him in the gut then and had nearly brought him to his knees months after that when he watched that North Korean guard shoot her.

He'd had his next assignment to distract him after his second, more permanent loss of Rikki, but his leave had sent him spiraling out of control. How much longer he could've gone on like that if Rikki hadn't shown up on his doorstep two nights ago, he hadn't a clue.

This time, as he faced his third abandonment by Rikki, he'd be ready. She'd survived. That was all that mattered to him.

He caressed her outer thighs and whispered, "Do you want me to go on? I can do a mean foot massage that could put any pedicurist to shame."

Her only response was a long, drawn-out sigh.

He stopped, his hands hovering above her legs.

He slid off the bed and crouched beside it, his face close to Rikki's, nose to nose.

Her long lashes fluttered, and her lips parted on a minty breath.

That was the first time he'd ever put Rikki Taylor to sleep…and it gave him a good feeling. He drew the sheet up to her shoulders and climbed into bed next to her.

She shifted onto her side, facing him, and he stroked the side of her full breast.

He murmured the words he'd never say to her out loud. "Love you."

She mumbled something, and Quinn's heart skipped a beat. Had she heard him and responded in kind?

"What?" He held his breath until he realized she was fast asleep.

She spoke in her sleep again, and this time he heard the word and repeated it. "Bell?"

Her mouth curved into a soft, sweet smile, and he kissed the tip of his finger and touched her bottom lip.

He didn't hear any bells, but he didn't have to. He knew how he felt about Rikki…even if she wanted to keep denying her own feelings for him.

And he'd do whatever it took to make her happy—with or without him.

THEY SPENT THE following day getting two credible CIA badges and a handful of matching business cards with Quinn's temp cell phone number, shopping for some convincing clothes to wear and holing up in the air-conditioned motel room.

Watching TV from the bed, Rikki crossed her legs at her ankles and tapped her bare feet together. "The small glimpses I'm getting of the city make me want to see more of it. The architecture is incredible, and I'm itching to tour some of those homes."

"We'll put Savannah on your list the next time you come out to New Orleans and do a two-for-one. I'll even throw in Nashville."

"I'll take you up on it." She drew her knees to her chest and wrapped one arm around her legs. "That was some massage last night. Totally relaxing."

"I aim to please." He touched two fingers to his forehead.

"I'm sorry I fell asleep. I mean…"

"Proved you wrong, didn't I?"

"You did?"

"You didn't think I could give you a massage without jumping your bones."

She balanced her chin on her knees. "I didn't mean to imply you were a caveman with no self-control. It's that our relationship before…"

"Was purely physical?" He shrugged. "Maybe for you."

Her eyes widened. "We didn't have that much time in Dubai."

"It was enough time for me, Rikki. You don't think I know what I want in a woman? What qualities are important to me?"

The panicked look on her face stopped him cold.

"You know what? We should start getting ready if we want to greet Belinda Dawson when she gets home from work. We don't want to give her too much time to go out again."

"You're right, although I dread putting on that suit." She rolled from the bed and grabbed a jacket from the back of the chair.

"You and me both." He ripped the plastic from the cheap, off-the-rack suit he'd bought earlier that day. "Do you know you talk in your sleep?"

"I do?" She froze and clutched the jacket to her chest, her pale face a shade lighter than the light beige of the suit. "What did I say?"

"I honestly don't remember." He just knew it hadn't been his name or any form of endearment for him. "Okay, I'm gonna put this thing on—if you think you can control yourself while I change."

She laughed a little too loudly. "That's fair."

He dropped his shorts to the floor and pulled on the polyester slacks. "Are you nervous about this?"

"David and I used to do stuff like this all the time. It's a snap."

"I'm not David. Are you afraid I'm going to screw it up?"

"You'll be fine. You're a quick learner."

Forty minutes later as Quinn drove his car, which had developed a rattle, down the gracious streets of Savannah's historic district, Rikki poked him in the side.

"You're going to have to park this jalopy a few blocks away. There is no way David's wife is going to believe the CIA is paying her an official visit in this little death trap."

Quinn ducked his head and peered at the palatial homes behind the live oaks dripping with Spanish moss. He whistled through his teeth. "Either David was making a lot more money than you at the Agency or he had a ton of life insurance. Did you say this was a new address for Belinda?"

"Yeah." Rikki rolled down the window and took a deep breath. "Smells lovely out here."

"Where did they live before?"

"Not in this neighborhood. I looked up David's old address and it wasn't near here, so the widow purchased some new digs after her husband's untimely death."

Glancing at the GPS, Quinn said, "Her house is up ahead on the right. I'm going to pull up alongside this park. Can you check the signs?"

"Slow down." Rikki stuck her head out the window. "It's okay to park here."

Quinn pulled up to the curb and unfolded himself from the car. "Can you please grab my jacket from the back?"

Rikki joined him on the sidewalk, jacket in hand. "Here you go."

They walked the two blocks to Belinda Dawson's house. Quinn's hand swung at his side so close to Rikki's, they kept brushing knuckles. He resisted the urge to grab her hand.

What would they do after this dead end? What would Rikki do? Where else would she go to find answers? He wanted to send her back to Jamaica and continue the investigation on his own. He had sources at the CIA—better sources than the hapless Jeff. He might be able to track this down for her. It might even be a good idea for Rikki to turn herself in and cooperate with the investigation.

He slid a glance at her firm jaw and long stride. No way. She wouldn't go down that road, and he didn't blame her. If the powers that be at the CIA thought they had their woman a year ago, what would change their mind this time? The fact that she'd spent time in a North Korean labor camp wouldn't convince them.

"There it is." Rikki tugged on his sleeve. "And there's a Lexus in the driveway, so she's probably home."

"Home and livin' large."

She drove a knuckle into his back. "You act like she's happy her husband's dead and would rather have the money."

"David Dawson was a snake. You should know that better than anyone. He wanted to cheat on his wife…with you. You don't really believe that garbage he was spewing about how Belinda didn't understand him. That's the oldest line in the book."

"I know that."

"And if you were so quick to peg David as a traitor based on the flimsy evidence of a fictional character, deep down you knew David was a snake."

"All right, all right." She put her finger to her lips

as they approached the wrought iron gate ringing the house. "It's time to keep your thoughts to yourself."

Quinn pushed down on the handle of the gate. "Whew, not locked. Ready, Agent Reid?"

"Copy, Agent Miller."

Once on the broad porch, Quinn rang the doorbell, which resounded somewhere deep in the house. "I wouldn't be surprised if a maid in a frilly apron answered the door."

"Or a butler."

A soft voice with a honeyed Southern accent floated out to the porch over an intercom. "Who is it? Press the white button, please."

Quinn reached for the speaker to the right of the doorbell and jabbed the button with his thumb. He laid his own Nawlins accent on thick. "Good evening, ma'am. I'm Agent Miller and this is Agent Reid. We've come to collect Agent Dawson's equipment."

At first Quinn thought she was going to ignore them and shut them out. Then the soft drawl responded, "Equipment?"

"I'm sorry, ma'am. The Agency contacted you about some equipment of Agent Dawson's and you indicated you had it at home?"

"I don't remember that." The locks on the door clicked, and it inched open.

A petite woman with fluffy blond hair appeared in the doorway.

Rikki stuck out her hand. "Mrs. Dawson? I'm

Agent Reid. Sorry for any confusion. We were sent to pick up some equipment."

Belinda released a measured sigh. "Sometimes I wonder how the government functions. Please come in."

Quinn took the attractive woman's soft hand in his. "Sorry for your loss, ma'am, and sorry for the red tape."

"It's been over a year. I'm used to it." She closed the door and folded her hands in front of her. "Can I get you some tea? Lemonade?"

"I'd love some tea, ma'am." Quinn slathered on the Southern charm. A woman like Belinda Dawson would expect it. A quick glance around the lavishly appointed living room marked Belinda as a woman who spared herself no comfort or reward.

Rikki shook her head. "Nothing for me, thank you. You have a beautiful home."

"Thank you." Belinda started for the kitchen and glanced over her shoulder. "I'll get it for you myself. The help has gone home for the day."

When she entered the vast kitchen, Quinn exchanged a quick look with Rikki, who raised her eyebrows.

Belinda returned to the room, carrying two glasses of tea, the ice clinking softly. As she handed one glass to Quinn, she said, "Equipment, you say?"

"Yes, when we…lose an agent, we do an inventory of his equipment. A few pieces were missing from Agent Dawson's effects. Agent Reid and I received notification that you'd been contacted and had located the missing equipment."

"You know, it's completely possible." Belinda aimed her big blue eyes at Quinn over the rim of her glass as she took a sip of the very sweet tea. "There was so much…red tape when David died. Did you know him?"

"I did not have the pleasure, ma'am." At least Quinn could be truthful about something.

"Agent Reid?" Belinda had approached Rikki from behind, hovering over her shoulder as Rikki studied a vast array of framed photographs on a shelf.

Rikki cranked her head over her shoulder. "No, I never met Agent Dawson, but then our paths wouldn't have crossed. I'd heard he was an incredible agent, though. A real treasure to the Agency."

Belinda bowed her head. "That's nice to hear. It's too bad he was betrayed by the one person he trusted the most."

Quinn's heart hammered as he watched Rikki across the room. *C'mon, Agent Reid, keep it together.*

"Oh?" Rikki tipped her head and her dark ponytail swung behind her. "I'd heard he was killed by the North Koreans."

"He was, but his partner made that happen. Rikki Taylor." She spit out the name as if it were poison on her tongue. "They were partners. He was her mentor. He taught her everything. She tried to seduce him first, and when that didn't work she betrayed him to the North Koreans. But she got hers. I heard she died, too. I don't know how or when, but it gave me some measure of satisfaction."

Rikki blinked. "I can imagine it would. We didn't hear that story."

Quinn ground his back teeth together. Dawson was worse than a snake if he told his wife Rikki had been trying to seduce him. Belinda probably found some evidence of David's infatuation with his partner, and he turned it around on Rikki.

Rikki picked up a picture from the shelf. "Is this Agent Dawson?"

Quinn had uncoiled his muscles enough to move toward the two women. He wanted a firsthand look at the snake himself. He'd only ever seen him at a distance when he first met Rikki in Dubai.

Belinda took the framed photo from Rikki's hands and traced a finger over the form of a fit, compact man in his midforties, with the build of a long-distance runner, shirtless and standing in knee-deep water.

Belinda almost whispered. "This is Davey. This is the last picture I have of him. We'd taken a brief vacation to the Bahamas before he left for Dubai, and then North Korea."

Rikki sniffed. "I'm so sorry, Mrs. Dawson. We didn't come here to bring up painful memories. If you don't have Agent Dawson's equipment, we can write it off as a misunderstanding."

"I can pretty much confirm I don't have any of Davey's work equipment here. I moved into this house about nine months ago—too many memories in the old place—and I would've remembered seeing anything of Davey's from work and moving it over with me."

"We'll report that, ma'am. Don't concern yourself." Quinn raised his glass before finishing off the tea. "That sure hit the spot."

Belinda placed Dawson's picture back on the shelf, caressing the edges of the frame. "If I do find something, is there a number where I can reach you?"

Quinn reached into his front pocket for his newly minted business cards and pulled one out. He pinched it between his fingers. "Here you go, ma'am. It's best to call my cell phone number."

"Well, I will certainly take a look." She made a half turn toward Rikki. "Are you sure you don't want some refreshment before you leave?"

"No, thank you. I feel bad that we troubled you on this wild-goose chase."

Belinda waved her hands. "Oh, Davey and I were married for over twenty years. I know how the Agency works."

A bead of sweat rolled down Quinn's back in his cheap suit, despite the chilly air in Belinda Dawson's house. Not only did this turn out to be a wild-goose chase for Rikki, she'd had to listen to David's slights and lies.

As Belinda walked them to the front door, she asked, "Are you taking any time to see the city? I do volunteer work at the Savannah Historical Society every weekday morning, and we have an incredible selection of artifacts and can give you some good sightseeing suggestions."

Rikki shook her head, her ponytail waving from side to side. "I'm afraid it's business only for us."

Quinn smiled. "Thanks again, ma'am."

Belinda opened the front door and turned to shake their hands again. "Have a nice trip back to…Washington."

They didn't say a word to each other as they walked down the pathway to the front gate and into the still night, light from the setting sun playing peekaboo between the trailing tails of Spanish moss.

When they hit the sidewalk out of sight of the house, Quinn took Rikki's arm. "Sorry about that."

"Sorry?" She turned toward him, her eyes alight with sparks. "I couldn't be happier with the results."

He tripped to a stop. "You enjoy getting trashed and vilified?"

"Small price to pay for the truth and the first big break in my investigation."

"You lost me."

"Quinn." She grabbed his lapels. "David Dawson is still alive."

Chapter Ten

Quinn's eyes popped open. "What are you talking about? How did you come to that conclusion?"

Rikki looked over his shoulder. She didn't trust Belinda Dawson one iota. "Let's keep moving. She could be calling the CIA or your cell phone number as we speak."

Quinn continued on the sidewalk, excitement lengthening his stride so that she had to hold on to his arm to keep up with him.

With a slight pant, she said, "It was that picture."

"The vacation picture from the Bahamas?"

"That wasn't the Bahamas. Did you get a load of that water? Looked like some muddy rice paddy in Southeast Asia."

"You're saying that's a recent picture of David? One taken after his supposed death in North Korea?"

"That's exactly what I'm saying."

"How could you possibly know that? Because of an imagined rice paddy?"

"Wait for the car. I'm not blabbing this on the sidewalk, even if there is nobody else around."

By the time they reached the car, sweat was dampening Rikki's back. She ripped off her jacket, and Quinn did the same.

Once in the car with the engine and the air running, Rikki bounced in her seat and turned toward Quinn. "It's not the place. It's the man and more specifically the tattoo."

"That tattoo on his chest? He didn't have that before?"

"Nope. The last time I saw David, right before I witnessed his so-called murder at the hands of the North Koreans, he most definitely did not have a big tattoo on his chest—a tattoo of a phoenix, I might add."

"You've seen David Dawson's chest?"

Her cough turned into a laugh. "That's all you can focus on? Of course I've seen David's chest. You know how scorching it gets in Korea, and all the other hot spots we've been in around the world. You've been in some of the same hot spots. I've seen him without his shirt several times, and I can say unequivocally the man never had a tattoo. Why Belinda keeps that picture around is beyond me. Beyond stupid."

"You don't think it could've been one of those temporary tattoos, do you?"

Compressing her lips into a thin line, Rikki tilted her head. "Really? The man is forty-four, not eight."

Quinn pulled away from the curb, his brows creating a vee over his nose. "David set up this Korea trip for the two of you with the cover that he had a line on Vlad. That got him money and support from

Ariel. He engineered his own death, while fingering you as a traitor at the same time. Why you?"

Rikki's knees bounced. "Because of just that—the Vlad story was a cover and if nothing came of it, I'd be a witness."

"If nothing came of it, he could claim his sources fell through. Happens all the time."

Quinn snapped his fingers several times. "This trip was David's opportunity to turn, to go over to the other side. He fakes his death so nobody is looking for him, and he sets up his partner so she takes the fall for being the traitor…and he gets his revenge."

"Revenge?" Rikki's stomach dropped. "What do you mean by that?"

"Because you rejected him, Rikki. He kills a lot of birds with those stones."

"Oh my God." She wrapped her ponytail around her hand. "It was David all along. He set me up. Why? Who is he working for?"

"This has Vlad's fingerprints all over it. This wouldn't be the first time he turned an agent or someone on the inside. My buddy Miguel Estrada had to deal with that. He was betrayed in Afghanistan and captured. Vlad is a master of manipulation. It wouldn't surprise me at all if he'd worked on David. Did you get the full effect of Belinda's house? Do you really think life insurance money and a government pension are paying for that? It sounds like she quit her marketing job, too, and is volunteering her time."

"She knows. Of course she knows her husband's alive. He sent her that picture—maybe as

proof." Rikki smacked her hand against her knee.
"I should've taken that photo. I need to provide proof
that David's still alive—not in a North Korean labor
camp, not held captive, not suffering from amnesia
and wandering around South Korea—but alive and
well and functioning as a traitor to his country."

"Taking that picture would've been risky. Belinda
would've known it was missing and would've known
it was us."

"I need to get some proof."

"The decoding. Let me get my guy, Donovan
Chan, to work on David's emails. I think we can
take it to the bank that those messages contain some
incriminating information." Quinn wheeled into a
parking lot and squealed to a stop. "And if Dawson's
betrayal has anything to do with Vlad, we're going
to nail them both."

"I want that picture, Quinn. I'm sure I'm not the
only person who can testify to the fact that David
Dawson didn't have a tattoo when he went to North
Korea. If I can plant some doubt that he perished
in North Korea, maybe the CIA can start looking
into Belinda Dawson's finances. There might be an
offshore account or some other irregularities, but it
starts with that photo."

"We can't just steal the picture. We'll have to stage
it as a break-in, and we'll have to do it at night. God
knows how many butlers, housekeepers and gardeners
Belinda has around the house during the day."

"Tonight. We do it tonight."

"She'll know it's us."

"I don't care. Let her suspect. I'm only too happy to strike some fear into her heart—and David's." Crossing her arms, she hunched her shoulders. "I can't believe he turned on me, after everything we went through together."

"You know what I think?" Quinn put the car in gear and drove out of the parking lot. "I think if he had been successful in seducing you, he would've tried to lure you to the dark side with him. As devastated as I'm sure he was when you rejected him, that's not what pushed him over the edge. Guys like that are bad seeds. He would've turned anyway if the price was right."

"You're probably right." She tapped on the window. "Where are we going?"

"I'm starving. We're going to get something to eat before returning to the motel and changing into something more comfortable for breaking and entering."

"Can we please go out? I doubt we're going to run into Belinda Dawson at dinner, since she seemed to have something simmering on her stove when we were there. Nobody else knows we're here. Nobody knows I'm anywhere...just like David."

"I'll meet you halfway. We'll pick up some soul food and eat at the hotel pool."

"I guess it's better than fast food in the room." She turned toward him with a tilt to her head. "What exactly is soul food?"

Quinn quirked his eyebrows up and down. "Allow me to introduce you to its delights."

THE DELIGHTS OF soul food included lots of deep frying and lots of carbs. Rikki sucked down a big gulp of disgustingly sweet tea and curled her legs beneath her on the chaise longue by the pool. She yawned. "So, soul food is a sleep aid, because the only thing I want to do right now is close my eyes and drift off."

Quinn rubbed and then patted his flat stomach. "Pretty good, huh?"

"Delish." Rikki eyed his trim waistline.

How did he manage to put away all that food and still look like a Greek god? She'd pay him the compliment, but she didn't want to get caught up in a discussion of food and weight and start Quinn wondering about all her new soft spots. He seemed to like them, anyway.

She pressed her hands against her own belly and the butterflies taking wing there. She'd tell Quinn about Bella as soon as she got the proof on David. Maybe she'd even let someone else take over the investigation, as long as the CIA didn't want to take her into custody.

Rikki swept up the used napkins on the table between them and shoved them into one of the plastic bags. "I have my clothes all picked out—black leggings, black T-shirt and a pair of sneakers for a quick getaway."

"And I have all my burglar tools. Should be a cinch to break in there—as long as she doesn't have an alarm system. If she has one of those, it'll take a little longer."

Rikki clambered out of the chaise longue and

dumped their trash in the bin by the gate. "I should be able to tell if she does have an alarm system and if it's armed."

"If it is, I got that covered." He held up a deep-fried ball of something. "Do you want the last one?"

"Knock yourself out."

They returned to the room and changed into their night-crawler outfits.

Standing before the mirror, Rikki wound the elastic holder around her ponytail once more. "Wish we had your motorcycle for this little assignment, or better yet, my silent electric scooter."

"We'll be fine. I'll leave the car by the park again. We'll get in there, swipe the picture and get out. Who knows? Belinda may not even notice it's missing for a day or two."

"Wait." Rikki spun around from the mirror. "I thought we were going to steal a few more things to make it look like a break-in."

"Do you really want to steal some woman's jewelry and small electronics?"

"You don't seriously expect me to feel some sympathy for a traitor and his wife, do you?"

"I'm not a thief."

"It would be extremely odd for a burglar to steal a framed photograph only. You're the one who made this point earlier." She wedged a hand on her hip. "Why are you having an attack of conscience now?"

"Okay, we'll take a few other things and then return them to…someone."

"Whatever you want to do. We should return them to the CIA for the secrets David probably stole."

"We'll figure it out." Quinn hitched a small backpack over one shoulder. "Are you ready?"

"Oh, yeah."

They didn't say much on the way over, and Rikki focused her private thoughts on David and his behavior their last year together. He had changed, had become less open with her. She'd written this change off to the awkwardness after his declaration of love for her and his anger when he found out about her and Quinn. Because he had been angry. Had that set him on this course?

No. He had to have arranged the North Korea trip prior to Dubai. Quinn was right. David already had the inclination to betray his country; whether that came from greed or disagreements with the country's policies, she couldn't tell, and it didn't matter anyway. There could be no valid excuse.

Quinn parked the car and cut the engine. "Do you think we should give it another hour? It's not much past midnight. What if she's a night owl?"

"She's not. She turns in early. I remember David telling me that—it was supposedly another point of contention between them, since he liked to stay up late and sleep in when he wasn't working, and Belinda preferred the opposite."

Quinn snorted. "Yeah, because that's a good reason to cheat on someone and end a marriage."

"That was probably all a lie. He probably just wanted to compromise me to use me. I'm sure he never loved me. If Belinda is okay with his deceit and is happy to spend his blood money, they're made for each other."

He clasped the back of her neck and squeezed it gently. "It's not you. Dawson would've betrayed any partner."

"Okay, let's do this." She dropped her head to the side and kissed his wrist.

The night air was heavy with the scent of magnolias from the park, and the sweet smell reminded her of the fragrant blooms in Jamaica and nights spent cradling Bella in the rocking chair in Mom's garden.

What was she doing here? She yearned to be back with her baby. She yearned to tell Quinn all about their daughter.

But she couldn't live her life as a dead woman.

It didn't take long for Quinn to break into Belinda's house. In an odd stroke of luck, Belinda hadn't enabled her alarm system.

They stepped through the side door and Rikki held her breath as she looked around the living room where they'd been earlier this evening. Low lights from beneath the kitchen counters gave a soft glow to the room, and they didn't even have to use their flashlights. What a nice welcome.

Rikki made a beeline for the built-in bookshelf and tripped to a stop. With her gloved fingers, she tapped the empty space that David's picture had occupied.

She gestured to Quinn, still hovering by the door.

He ducked next to her, and she whispered in his ear, "The picture is gone."

He swept the light from his phone across the photos on the shelves and swore softly under his breath. "I don't like this, Rikki. We need to get out."

Her heart jumped, mimicking the urgency in his voice. "Wh-why?"

"It's all too convenient for us—the alarm system, the lights and now the missing picture. It's almost like she expected us."

"Then why would she make it easy for us?"

"To lure us in." He grabbed her arm. "We're done here."

Rikki twisted her head around for one last, longing look at that bookshelf as Quinn pulled her toward the side door—the door that hadn't been double-locked.

What had Belinda done with that incriminating picture? Had she realized the stupidity of showing it to a couple of CIA agents? Belinda had probably figured nobody would do a before-and-after comparison of her dead husband's chest.

Quinn hustled Rikki through the side door, and eased it closed. As soon as the door clicked, Rikki heard another click.

"Get your hands up where I can see them."

Chapter Eleven

A shot of adrenaline pumped through Quinn's body and he dropped to the ground, making a grab for Rikki's legs to take her down with him. But Rikki was two steps ahead of him, already on the ground and army-crawling toward the back of the house.

A beam of light swept the space above them, bouncing off the door they'd just passed through.

Staying low, Quinn lunged around the same corner where Rikki had just disappeared. His gun dug into his ribs. He left it there. Although any cop worth his salt would've lit up the scene by now with more than just a flashlight, Quinn couldn't be sure that the Savannah PD *didn't* have them at gunpoint. It could very well be some rookie cop on the other side of that click.

Whoever it was hadn't given them a second order. He probably couldn't see them with the clouds wafting across the crescent moon and no lights illuminating the side of the house. That was another convenience Belinda had afforded them. She might have lured them to the dark side of the house, but she'd also just given them an advantage.

Neither of them spoke, but Quinn could hear Rikki's short spurts of breath as she dragged herself up to a crouching position.

She jabbed his shoulder and pointed to the fence.

A semicircle of light awaited them on their way to that fence, but Quinn didn't want to give their pursuer a shot at them once he rounded the corner.

He shook his head at Rikki and jerked his thumb over his shoulder at the stealthy rustle behind them. A seasoned cop would've called backup by now, but Quinn couldn't be 100 percent sure that Belinda hadn't called the police, and he didn't want to risk tangling with a member of law enforcement—especially since he and Rikki had been caught red-handed breaking and entering.

A body of water to his left caught a glimmer of light from the slice of moon as it emerged from a rolling cloud cover. Quinn tugged on Rikki's pant leg and tipped his chin toward the pond. Even if they made a splash going into the water, the man with the gun wouldn't be able to get a clear line of sight on them—not like he would once he came around that corner with his flashlight.

Rikki didn't need any encouragement from him. On her hands and knees, she crawled to the edge of the pond and slipped in headfirst.

Quinn rolled in after her and kept his body flat. The pond had enough water to cover them, but only if they stretched out their bodies and kept low. Now all they needed was a couple of reeds to poke up above the surface of the water to breathe.

He and Rikki floated and bobbed side by side, submerged in the murky water until they reached the far end of the pond.

They'd have to head over the back fence and make a run for it if they hoped to get out of this situation. He squeezed Rikki's arm.

Again, she knew what had to be done.

She breached the surface first, emerging from the water like some slinky, primordial creature, and he scrambled over the slippery edge behind her. The noise of their escape broke the silence of the night, and the light from the flashlight made a jerky survey above the pond.

By the time the beam of light found Quinn, Rikki had launched herself over the fence. As Quinn grabbed the slats of wood to freedom, their assailant fired his first shot—from a silencer.

The bullet cracked the fence inches from Quinn's right hand. That was all the incentive he needed. He hoisted himself over and landed on the ground.

Rikki grabbed the back of his shirt at the collar. "Run."

"No kidding."

They'd landed in someone else's backyard, but Quinn couldn't even see the house from their position. Belinda had bought herself a place on a large lot, alongside other homes on equally large lots. The size of these yards would save their necks.

In a crouch, they ran for the fence to their left.

The clouds cooperated with them and drifted across the slice of moon again.

Rikki hit the fence with both hands. "I can't get over this without a boost. Can you?"

"Piece of cake, Buttercup." He laced his fingers together, and Rikki wedged the sole of her tennis shoe against his palms. "Ready?"

"Just hurry it up."

He launched her up, and she hoisted herself over.

His height gave him an advantage, and he swung over the fence with ease.

They made their way through a couple more lawns like that before hitting the street. Their shoes squishing with water, they kept to the shadows until they reached the park.

Rikki was panting by the time she grabbed the door handle of his vehicle. "It's a good thing we left the car down here."

"Yep, but I'm surprised Belinda Dawson didn't provide a getaway car for us."

Quinn started the engine before he fully sat down or closed the door. He left the lights off as he crawled into the street, checking his rearview mirror.

The cars on the streets of Savannah were few and far between until they emerged from the quiet residential streets into a boulevard dotted with bars and nightspots.

Quinn finally let out a pent-up breath, but still kept watch on his mirrors.

Rikki slumped in her seat, pressing a hand over her heart and the wet T-shirt that stuck to her chest.

"That was close. He was no cop, was he? Did you get a look at him?"

"I didn't see him at all, but you're right. I don't think Belinda called the cops on us." Quinn sluiced his wet hair back from his forehead and combed out a piece of moss.

"Then who did she call? Who was that? He had a silencer." Rikki crossed her arms over her midsection. "It must've been CIA. She called the Agency to check on us and discovered nobody had been sent for David's equipment."

"Maybe, but how did someone get here so quickly and why the subterfuge?" Quinn rubbed his palms, which the fence had abraded, against the steering wheel. "If she called the CIA, found out we were impostors and then reported us, why would she collude with the Agency to catch us in the act? The CIA would never use a spouse like that to lure impostors out of the woodwork. Especially a widow. Can you imagine the liability if the Agency did that and a spouse wound up dead?"

"It could've been someone from the Agency but not sanctioned by the Agency. Is that what you mean? Someone already out here looking after Belinda. Someone who's in on the joke and knows that David is alive and well and getting tattooed in Thailand, or wherever." Rikki grabbed her ponytail and twisted it to wring out the pond water.

"That's what I'm thinking, someone with the Agency—or not, but nobody official."

Rikki tucked a wet strand of hair behind her ear.

"That's a scarier scenario than having an on-duty agent after us."

"Except—" Quinn wheeled into the parking lot of their motel and parked in front of their room "—if an agent had captured us, taken us down at gunpoint, the Agency would've wasted no time identifying you, unless you erased your fingerprints with acid, but I recall your fingertips being intact."

She wiggled her fingers in front of her. "The hair and the eyes are as far as I'll go for a disguise. I'm going to agree with you and bet our shooter was either a rogue agent working with David or someone involved in this traitorous network of David's jumping on any hint that someone believes he's still alive."

Quinn cut the engine and lights but didn't make a move to leave the car. "Which brings us back to Belinda."

"It sure seemed like she trusted us while we were there. What do you think set off her alarm bells?"

"Maybe the interest in the photo. She realized after we left that the picture was of David post-death and started to get worried."

Rikki leveled a finger at him, seemingly in no hurry to get out of the car and her wet clothing. "Or she called the number on your fake card."

He tapped the burner phone in his cup holder. "Except I didn't get any calls on this phone."

"Either I showed too much interest in that picture or she had orders from David to be wary of any outreach from the Agency. She called the CIA to check out our story."

"Our story didn't pass the test. She brushed it off with the Agency and then made a call to her henchman."

"And set us up." Rikki rubbed her chin. "How did she know we'd be back?"

"She didn't know for sure, or Dawson is so paranoid he orchestrated the setup just to be on the safe side."

"Do you think she called David after we left?"

"Makes sense, doesn't it? Isn't that something David would do? Disable the alarm system, leave off the lights on one side of the house, disengage one set of locks on the door and have Belinda call in backup when we showed up. Hell—" he yanked the door handle "—she might've had a camera watching our every move down there."

Back in the room, Rikki peeled off her wet T-shirt and shimmied out of the jeans sticking to her thighs. "Ugh, that pond water was disgusting. I hope you didn't swallow any of it."

"My lips were sealed. I'm just glad we left our phones in the car. I would've had a lot of explaining to do to get my encrypted phone replaced."

Rikki kicked her wet clothes into a corner. "We need to get David's emails to Chan and decoded. I want to know what he was up to and what he was doing in South Korea."

"Other than setting up his own death and your entrapment? I'd say Dawson was a busy boy—and I already sent the emails to Chan."

"Why South Korea? There must've been a reason

for him to pick that area instead of staging all this in Dubai, for example."

"That's a mystery those messages might solve." Quinn pulled his own damp T-shirt over his head and tossed it into Rikki's wet pile of clothes. "Right now I want to get this pond scum off my body. Do you want to help me?"

"I'd like nothing more than to rub pond scum from your body."

Quinn sprinted past Rikki to the bathroom before she could change her mind. He ran a warm bath and dumped some body wash in the water to create bubbles. Then he stripped off the rest of his clothes and sank into the tub, as much as his six-foot-three frame could sink.

"That was fast—bubbles and everything." Rikki hung on the door frame in her underwear.

"Technically it's body wash, but it worked." He scooped up a handful of bubbles and blew on them.

"I knew navy SEALs were resourceful. I just didn't realize in how many ways." She stepped out of her panties and unhooked her bra.

Quinn opened his legs, patting the water between them. "I have a place for you right here."

Rikki dipped a toe in the water before stepping in and lowering herself into the tub. Leaning back against his chest, she said, "Don't get any ideas in here, McBride. We might both end up drowning."

"Ideas?" He cupped her breasts from behind and nuzzled her neck. "What ideas do you think I might have?"

She put one arm behind her, winding it around his neck. "The kinds of ideas you have every time we're within two feet of each other."

"Can I help it if I find you irresistible?"

And then he used all his resourcefulness to show her.

THE FOLLOWING MORNING, Quinn got back to business. While Rikki looked through her old emails from David, Quinn contacted Donovan Chan again. If Chan wondered why Quinn was asking about a dead agent, he kept his questions to himself.

Rikki looked up from Quinn's laptop. "I don't see anything suspicious in David's communications, nothing to suggest that our mission to Korea was anything other than what he claimed—a lead on Vlad."

"Did he ever disclose how he got this intel?" Quinn tossed his phone on the cushion beside him.

Rikki wedged the tip of her finger between her teeth. "Not in the emails, but he mentioned a name when we were in Dubai, and it was the same guy we met in South Korea—Buddy Song."

"Was this Song in intelligence in South Korea? Why wouldn't Song go straight to the CIA or to Ariel and the Vlad task force?"

"I don't know." Rikki shrugged. "I didn't ask him. David had his contacts outside of our partnership, relationships he'd cultivated over the years before I even became an agent and started working with him."

"Do you know how to contact Song? Did anyone

ever reach out to him after David's supposed murder and your capture?"

"My supposed murder, too." She raised her eyebrows. "You know that better than anyone."

Quinn clasped the back of his neck and squeezed. "Do you have to keep reminding me?"

"Like I said before, if it hadn't been you I'd be dead." She tipped the computer from her lap onto the bed and crossed her legs. "Ariel didn't tell me what kind of investigation was done into David's murder, but I doubt anyone knows about Song. David didn't even put his name in an email to me. We only ever spoke about him."

"I think Song is a good place to start. What do you remember about him? Where did you meet?"

"We met in Seoul, at a park. He spoke English very well. He helped us cross the border, and I got the feeling it wasn't his first rodeo."

"He was probably someone who facilitated border crossings between North and South Korea. Maybe that was his insight into Vlad. He probably helped him cross the border, too."

"Could be. Song got us to a tunnel between the two countries and said goodbye there. The rest is history. David and I crossed over and hadn't traveled five miles before I was taken and David killed—or so I thought."

"But now we know Song didn't set up David. David manipulated the entire scenario, with or without Song's knowledge."

"And definitely without mine."

Rikki rubbed her nose, and Quinn knew David's betrayal of her stung. He couldn't imagine any of his sniper teammates turning on him like that. For a while, the navy had tried to tell them Miguel Estrada had been working with the enemy, but he and the rest of the guys hadn't believed that for one second.

But Rikki had proof.

Quinn stood up and stretched his arms, almost brushing his fingertips on the ceiling. "Do you think Ariel can track down Song? Would she? She's deep undercover enough that nobody's following her movements."

"I can ask her. I never thought about him before, but that's when I believed our mission to Korea was something straightforward, or at least as straightforward as our missions ever were. Now that I know David pulled a scam on me—" she flicked her fingers in the air "—everything and everyone is fair game."

Quinn peered through the curtains on the window. "We can do all this on computers and on my trusty phone. We don't need to stay in Savannah."

"When do you have to report back for duty?"

"Three weeks." A sudden fear gripped Quinn's heart. "If we can't clear you before then, you need to go back to Jamaica where you'll be safe."

Rikki's lashes dropped over her eyes. "Maybe. I vowed I wouldn't return there until my name was cleared."

"I can continue our sleuthing."

She widened her eyes. "From Afghanistan or

Pakistan or Libya or wherever you're going? I don't think so, Quinn."

In two steps, he was at the bed and sitting on the edge. "Then we'll figure it out, and then maybe you don't have to go back to Jamaica. You can go back to your job and I can do mine and maybe we can be together—freewheeling and fancy-free, no strings, nothing to tie us down except each other."

Rikki sucked in her lower lip. "That's what you want?"

"That's what I always wanted. I don't understand why I scared you off in Dubai to the point you felt you had to run away. Yeah, I felt something deep for you, maybe deeper than you felt yourself, but that never meant I wanted to restrict you, make you give up the job you love. Hell, my job isn't exactly a nine-to-five, white-picket-fence deal."

"We have to talk this through first." Rikki twisted her fingers. "There's a lot I have to tell you."

"About your time in the labor camp and your escape?" He cupped his hand over one of her knees. "I do want to hear about that, Rikki. It'll only make me think you're more amazing than I already do."

"It's not just that, Quinn. Jamaica…"

"You're not going to tell me you have a boyfriend in Jamaica, are you?" He curled his fingers into her leg. "I don't even care. I know I love you more than anyone else could."

She pressed her fingers against her bottom lip and whispered, "Quinn."

"So whatever it is…" He jerked his head toward

the ringing phone on the table by the window. "That's not my regular phone. That's the burner, and nobody has that number except Belinda."

"Or random telemarketers."

Quinn pushed himself off the bed and lunged for the phone. "It's her."

He jabbed the button to answer and to put the phone on speaker at the same time. "Hello? Agent Miller."

"Agent Miller, this is Belinda Dawson."

"Mrs. Dawson, did you find some of your husband's equipment after all?" He rolled his eyes at Rikki, who'd followed him off the bed and had her hip wedged against the table.

"Let's cut to the chase, Miller, if that's really your name."

Quinn swallowed. "Pardon me, ma'am?"

"You can cut the Southern boy charm, too. I'm immune."

"I'm afraid you lost me, Mrs. Dawson."

"I almost lost you last night to that thug watching my house night and day."

Rikki grabbed his wrist, her eyes taking up half her face.

"You're going to have to explain yourself, Mrs. Dawson."

"You and I both know my husband is alive, Agent Miller, and I can give you the proof you need."

Chapter Twelve

Rikki clapped a hand over her mouth. Why was Belinda doing this? Why was she outing David?

Quinn braced his hands on the table and hunched over the phone. "Why would you give me proof that your husband is alive?"

"That's what you were sniffing around here for, wasn't it? You and your...partner seemed awfully interested in that photo of David—the one taken after his supposed death. When you zeroed in on that picture, I finally felt a glimmer of hope."

Quinn raised his eyebrows at Rikki, but all she could do was shrug. She had no idea where Belinda was going with this.

Quinn cleared his throat. "What do you mean by hope? Hope for what?"

"David swore me to secrecy about his betrayal. He warned me that I'd lose everything if the CIA found out he'd been spying for the enemy. He sent people to watch me, to keep tabs on me."

"How do you know my partner and I aren't just two more watchdogs?"

Rikki nodded at Quinn. He knew all the right questions—the same ones she'd be asking.

"You were fishing. They don't fish. Your unexpected appearance on my doorstep yesterday told me that the CIA has doubts about David's story."

Rikki scribbled a question on a napkin and shoved it toward Quinn.

He gave her a thumbs-up. "Why didn't you just call the CIA yourself and report this?"

"You're kidding." Belinda gave a soft snort. "You work for the Agency, so you should understand. I don't know whom to trust over there. I didn't know who was in on it, or even if his fake death had been sanctioned by someone over there. I wasn't about to step out of line, but you two…"

Quinn cut her off and with a gruff voice asked, "If you trusted us so much, why did you call the dogs on us last night?"

Belinda released a long sigh. "That wasn't me."

"The alarm system, the lights, the door? You even took the picture."

"They ordered me to do all that. They knew you'd been there." She sobbed. "They bugged my house."

Quinn's gaze locked on to Rikki's. "And now? How do you know you're not being bugged now?"

"I bought a throwaway phone, and I'm at a restaurant waiting to have brunch with my friend. David taught me well."

Rikki couldn't contain herself anymore. "Why are you turning on your husband now, Mrs. Dawson?"

Belinda sucked in a quick breath over the line.

"I'm tired of living this way. David was supposed to send for me, but he hasn't. I can't trust anyone. I don't want to get on the bad side of the CIA and be tried as a traitor. I'd be willing to…you know, testify against him to save myself."

Rikki avoided Quinn's warning looks and plunged ahead. "At the beginning of the call, you said you had proof that David is alive. Is that the picture?"

"That and other things. I'll turn them over to you so you can go after him and I can be protected. I *will* be protected, won't I?"

Clamping a hand on Rikki's shoulder, Quinn answered the desperate wife. "I think we can work something out. How do you propose to get us this proof if you're under such close watch?"

"There are ways. I have a lot of old friends in this town, and I socialize quite frequently. In fact, I'm meeting old friends tonight for cocktails. If Agent Reid were to stop by our table, just another Savannah socialite…or friend of my husband's, who would question that?"

Quinn shook his head at her, and Rikki put her finger to her lips. "Let's hear the plan, Mrs. Dawson."

As Belinda laid out her scheme to pass off proof that David had faked his death, Quinn peppered her with questions and Rikki took a few notes.

When she finished, Belinda said, with a hitch in her voice, "I really want to do this. I need to think about myself now."

"I'll be there, Mrs. Dawson."

Quinn ended the call and tapped the edge of the phone against his chin. "Why should we trust her?"

"Because her reasoning sounds plausible."

"What if it's a trick to get us on someone's radar?"

"If it is, we can outmaneuver them. We did it last night when we weren't even expecting a trap. This time we'll be even more on our guard and on our game. Besides—" she ran a hand down his tense back "—why would Belinda admit the truth about David being alive if she weren't on the up-and-up?"

Quinn's back got even stiffer. "It wouldn't matter... if she planned to have us killed."

Rikki's hand stopped midcircle where she was rubbing Quinn's back. "I need this proof, Quinn. Nobody is going to believe me, or worse yet, some anonymous tip that Agent David Dawson is a traitor who faked his own death."

"Ariel will believe you. Take this to her and let her launch an investigation."

"There's no denying Ariel is pretty untouchable in the intelligence community, but she has her hands full running the Vlad task force."

"You said it yourself, Rikki. We could make a good case that this *is* about Vlad."

"A good case? A string of undeciphered, coded emails and the word of a disgraced CIA agent, presumed dead?" She slid her hand down his arm and entwined her fingers with his. "I have to do this, Quinn. I won't be by myself, right? You'll be there to look out for me."

"I don't like it, Rikki. I know better than anyone

that a sniper can pick you off at a distance and we wouldn't realize it until it was too late."

"Then you also know better than anyone that I can get in and out of that restaurant undercover. With you on my side, no sniper or shooter is going to get a chance at me."

"I think you're exaggerating my talents." He turned and wedged a knuckle beneath her chin. "I'll get you inside that bar, and then you have one drink or whatever Belinda has planned, get the proof and get out of there."

"I think it'll work, and it's not possible for me to exaggerate your talents."

"I'm just glad you decided to forgive me so that I could help you with all this. Not that you're not a kick-ass agent, but at least two people need to be doing this job and I think we make a great team." He raised her hand to his lips and kissed the back of it.

She rested her head against his shoulder. They *did* make a good team, and she planned to tell him just how much they were going to be a team to raise their daughter—as soon as they got past this danger.

A few hours after dinner, Rikki slipped on taupe sling-back heels and smoothed her beige skirt over her thighs. "What do you think? Do I look like a Southern belle born to privilege and debutante balls?"

"I don't know about all that, but you look beautiful." Quinn came up behind her and ran a hand through her hair. "I miss those riotous red curls, though, and how the sun would set them on fire. The last time I saw you…"

His fingers tightened in her hair, sending a tingle down her thighs.

Tipping her head into the curve of his palm, she whispered, "But that wasn't the last time you saw me. I'm here now. We both are."

He pressed a kiss against her temple. "Let's keep it that way. Are you sure you want to meet Belinda? It could be a trap. She could have someone waiting for us."

"I have to get my hands on this proof." She placed a finger over his lips. "Why would she want us out of the picture? She knows we don't have any other evidence that David is alive."

"Why did the guy last night taking shots at us want us out of the way?"

"Because if he's working with David, he doesn't know what we have. He doesn't know what Belinda told us. He was trying to eliminate a possible threat."

"Let's get this over with. I can see there's no talking you out of it. You might as well have that red hair on your head, because you're just as stubborn as a brunette."

"Red hair does not make you stubborn." She gave Quinn a playful push while a smile curved her lips as she thought about little red-haired Bella already trying to assert herself at nine months old.

Rikki grabbed a light sweater from the back of the chair and held it up. "Just in case they're blasting the air in the bar."

Before they left the hotel, Quinn called a car for her and saw her safely inside before heading for his own vehicle.

Rikki waved to him out the back window and settled in her seat with a sense of excitement buzzing through her veins. She'd been made for this work. If she could clear her name, how would she reconcile her career with motherhood? Bella meant more to her than anything in the world, more to her than a career—even this career.

And Quinn? How would he fit into it all? He'd been the one talking about forever when they were in Dubai, and that had rattled her. Now he'd changed his tune and had suggested they could both pursue their careers and meet up all over the world when they could. Now she had to break it to him that they had a child together.

She sighed and pressed her fingers against the window. "Almost there?"

"Just about. Ever been to Savannah Joe's before?"

"Nope."

"Nice place. You gotta try the mint juleps—best in the city."

"I'll do that. Thanks for the tip."

The driver pulled up in front of the restaurant-bar, and Rikki thanked him and slipped out of the back-seat. As Quinn had instructed, she ducked her head and made a beeline for the entrance. If someone had a rifle trained on the entrance to the restaurant, he'd have to recognize her first and set up a shot. She'd given him no time for that at all.

Stepping through the front door, she let out a breath. Belinda had explained the layout—a restaurant in front with tables behind large screened windows, and a busy bar in the back on the river.

As the hostess approached her, Rikki pointed to the back and then made her way to the large bar that separated the dining area from the cocktail lounge.

She rubbed her lips together, moistening her lipstick, and squared her shoulders as she stepped down into the bar area. She scanned the room, and Belinda's subtle wave caught her attention.

Quinn didn't have to worry about the setup. This bar, packed with people, didn't exactly lend itself to ambush and murder at the end of a sniper's rifle.

Rikki plastered a smile on her face and wended her way through the tables to reach Belinda and her two friends, crowded around a cocktail table.

Belinda half rose from her seat. "Here she is. Peyton, this is Melissa and Jordan. Ladies, Peyton, a friend of David's family."

"So nice to meet you." Rikki shared limp handshakes with the other two women and sat next to Belinda. "This is a great place. I heard the mint juleps are to die for."

"Have this one." Belinda shoved a tall glass with a spray of mint in front of Rikki. "I've already had one, and these two already ordered another round."

"Thank you." Rikki smoothed out the napkin beneath the sweating glass. She wanted to keep her wits about her tonight, get the photo and whatever else Belinda had, and get out. Quinn was supposed to be waiting at the back door of the restaurant to whisk her away once Belinda had handed off the proof in the ladies' room.

She'd let Belinda call the shots and make the move to the ladies' room, but this had to look like a legit social interaction in case anyone was watching Belinda.

"Looks refreshing." Rikki swirled the straw in her glass as the waitress delivered three more drinks.

The waitress raised her eyebrows at Rikki. "Can I get you something?"

"I'm good, thanks." Rikki tapped the glass and then almost choked when she glanced over the waitress's shoulder and saw Quinn sitting at the bar.

He had to see that she'd be safe here. She'd rather have him keeping watch outside, and she hoped Belinda hadn't noticed him.

"To friendships." Belinda raised her glass in the center of the table and the other two women held up their glasses, as well.

Rikki clinked her glass with theirs. "To friendships."

The women immediately launched into a discussion of some mutual acquaintance, ripping apart her parenting skills.

Rikki smirked. So much for friendships. She pulled the straw from the glass and sucked some liquid from the bottom of the straw—just a drop or two.

Rikki puckered her lips. She'd never had a mint julep before, and the tartness of the drink surprised her. The garnish on the drink didn't even include a slice of lime.

She stuck the straw back in the glass and took a tentative sip.

Rikki rolled the liquid on the surface of her tongue, and her nostrils flared as the sour smell reached her nose. The drink dribbled down the back of her throat, but Rikki froze, refusing to swallow.

David's voice floated across her consciousness, and she could picture him in the hotel room in Bangkok pinching a small vial between his fingers. "I discovered this here, Rikki, and it's very useful because it has an immediate impact but proceeds to incapacitate slowly and gradually. It also has a tart taste and smell that could pass for a citrus garnish on a cocktail."

Rikki convulsively clutched the hem of the tablecloth. The liquid had traveled too far for her to stop it unless she made a scene coughing it up.

So she allowed the poison to slide down her throat.

Chapter Thirteen

Quinn studied the four women over the rim of his beer mug. Rikki seemed to be doing a good job of acting like the long-lost friend. She laughed, chattered and sipped her mint julep along with the rest.

Did she forget this wasn't a social call? She needed to nudge Belinda along for their meeting in the john—if Belinda planned to stick with the scheme. He didn't trust the woman for a second.

"Another beer, sir?"

He waved off the bartender and plucked some bills from his pocket. Then from the corner of his eye, he sensed a commotion.

He jerked his head to the side to see Rikki stagger to her feet, almost upsetting her chair. His muscles coiled. His head swiveled from side to side. Nobody else had noticed.

Belinda rose from the table and placed a hand on Rikki's arm. Maybe this was the ruse to get them to the ladies' room.

Rikki leaned against Belinda while Belinda

laughed with the other women and curled an arm around Rikki's waist.

Quinn let out a breath. For a minute he thought Rikki might be injured, but the demeanor of the other two women didn't support this.

Belinda would take Rikki to the ladies' room, hand over the proof, and then they could get the hell out of here.

Quinn narrowed his eyes and followed their progress to the hallway at the back. His gaze shifted to Belinda's friends, still at the table.

He'd give Rikki and Belinda exactly thirty seconds before he went back there himself and hustled Rikki out of the bar. Just because she'd gotten in here without incident didn't mean they'd let her leave. Belinda could have someone waiting for them in the alley.

Quinn shoved himself off his barstool and strode to the back of the room. Turning the corner to the restrooms, he grazed shoulders with a man coming out of the men's room, and the hair on the back of his neck quivered.

Knots formed in his gut and he crashed into the ladies' room.

A woman washing her hands at the sink smirked. "Wrong place."

Quinn ignored her and peered under the first stall. Rikki hadn't been wearing short boots.

He pushed in the door of the next stall. "Rikki?"

A groan from the third stall answered him and he gave the door a shove. The door just missed Rikki propped up against the stall, her face white and twisted with pain.

"What happened? Where's Belinda?"

"Follow her. Just left. Get her."

"I'm not going anywhere. What the hell happened?"

"I'm okay. I'll be okay." She pressed her purse into his hands, her own shaking. "Get the ipecac."

He dumped the contents of her purse on the tile floor and grabbed a small brown bottle. "This stuff?"

She nodded. "Open."

He twisted off the cap and handed it to her. She placed it at her lips and threw some back. Almost immediately, she heaved.

"Out." She pushed him out of the stall.

Another woman had come in and hovered by the first stall. "Is she okay?"

The sound of vomiting came from Rikki's stall, and Quinn shrugged. "She's sick."

The woman wrinkled her nose. "Probably too many of those mint juleps."

Several minutes later, Rikki emerged from the stall, shoving her hair back from her face. She gave the woman at the sink a weak smile. "Sorry about that."

"Oh, honey, it was those mint juleps, wasn't it? Bourbon, powdered sugar." She stuck out her tongue. "Vile."

"You could say that." Rikki ran water over her hands in the sink and splashed her face and rinsed her mouth.

Quinn yanked several paper towels from the dispenser and handed them to her. "Feeling better?"

"Lots." She dabbed her face and neck with the paper towels and ducked back into the stall, ripping off a length of toilet paper. While she blew her nose and did another round of hand-washing, Quinn gathered the items from her purse off the floor and stuffed them back into her bag, including the bottle of ipecac. How the hell did she happen to have that? He studied the sharpened nail file, a bit of rope and another bottle of a clear substance before dropping each into her purse. Travel kit for a CIA agent on assignment?

Two other women had come into the restroom and Quinn apologized, explaining that his wife had been ill, but the women's presence didn't give him and Rikki a chance to talk. And they needed to talk.

Quinn took her arm and hunched over her as they exited the ladies' room. He placed a hand on the silver bar of the back door. "Stay down, crouch forward, stay next to the building."

Rikki cleared her throat. "I don't think we have to worry about anyone else. Belinda was lying about being followed. Besides, I'm supposed to be dead—again."

"Don't argue."

Quinn sneaked Rikki out the back door of the restaurant as if they had a team of snipers taking aim from all four corners of the alley.

He'd wedged his car behind a waitress's after paying her forty bucks for the privilege to get as close as possible to the restaurant. When he handed Rikki into the passenger seat, he said, "Stay down."

She complied, arms folded over her stomach, and he hoped she wouldn't have another episode in his car.

Checking all mirrors, he pulled out of the alley and drove for several blocks.

Rikki finally piped up. "We need to go after Belinda, Quinn."

"Can you tell me what happened now?"

"She poisoned me, slipped it in my mint julep. As soon as I figured out what I was drinking, I stopped drinking it. I wiped my mouth several times and spit the drink into a napkin. One time, I was able to pour out a bit on the floor."

His hands gripped the steering wheel. And he'd been worried about shooters outside the restaurant. "So that and the syrup of ipecac saved you. How'd you know to bring it, or is it standard operating procedure for you spooks?"

"Actually, David saved me."

"What?"

"I'd never had a mint julep before, but this one tasted nothing like I expected. It had a tart taste and smell, and then I remembered David showing me a poison he'd discovered in Thailand. Fast-acting to incapacitate the victim, but slow enough to delay actual death for a few days. Belinda didn't want me dropping dead at the table, but she also had no intention of giving me David's picture or any other proof."

"Did she tell you this as she led you away to the bathroom?"

"She didn't say much of anything. She kept up appearances to the end, soothing me and sympathizing—up until the moment she abandoned me in the bathroom stall and took off."

"She admitted David was alive because she planned to kill you and never turn over any evidence. But why go through all this to kill you? Why not call out one of David's henchmen, like she did at her house?"

"That didn't work because you were there."

"And why just you and not me? Unless she has something else planned for me."

"She probably does."

"But now I'm on my guard."

Rikki smacked the dashboard with both hands. "It's time to strike. She thinks I'm dead and you're running scared."

"This makes no sense to me, Rikki." Quinn plowed a hand through his hair. "If she had called in one of David's associates to take us out in the parking lot, or even if she never contacted us at all after the failed attempt at her house, both of those scenarios would compute better. Admitting David was alive? Luring you out to kill you with poison? I don't get it."

She pressed her hands against her bubbling

tummy. "We don't have to get it. We just have to get her. She thinks I'm dead. Part of my stumbling and staggering with her was an act to convince her of that fact. She's going to pass on the news of my demise to the men she has coming after us."

"I'm very much alive, and wouldn't I be coming right at the woman who killed my partner?"

"We'll take her by surprise, at her house."

Quinn tugged on his ear. "You're after the photo again. She's probably destroyed it by now. Maybe it's better if I set up a meeting with her. She knows I'm still alive."

"Then what? A meeting is not going to do any good if she doesn't bring proof that David is alive."

"Instead of a meeting—" Quinn drummed his thumbs against the steering wheel as he made the last turn to their motel "—I'll take her by surprise. I'll escort her someplace where we can have a private… conversation. You stay out of sight until the interrogation. I want to get to the bottom of this. I want her to explain her actions."

"I want that picture."

"I know you do." He rubbed her arm. "But we have to expect she destroyed it. Let's get some answers from her first."

"Where are you going to catch her off guard?"

Quinn parked the car and released his seat belt. "Despite her subterfuge on behalf of David, Belinda seems to go on with her life. We know she volunteers at the Savannah Historical Society in the mornings. I'll catch her when she's leaving her shift tomorrow morning. Just a friendly little talk."

"You don't believe someone's watching her?"

"Why would they? She's on David's side. She proved that tonight by trying to poison you." As that fact hit him all over again, he reached out to grab Rikki's hand. "I think she has an associate or two of David's close by that she can call out when she needs help, like setting us up last night, but I don't think they're keeping tabs on her. I doubt there was anyone there tonight."

"Just her and her little vial of poison." She pounded her knee with her fist. "I can't believe I fell for the oldest trick in the book."

"You didn't fall for it. You recognized the smell and taste of the poison and you took action. Your instincts are still good, kid."

She smiled at him before opening the door and slipping out of the car.

When they got to the motel room, Quinn checked his laptop. "Hey, I got a message from Chan on the decoding."

Rikki leaned over him, her hair fluttering against his cheek. "Can he do it?"

"He's going to try. He has some programs he's going to use."

"Fingers crossed." And then she crossed them.

He closed his hand around her crossed fingers and kissed the tips. "We're going to solve this and get you back into action—where you belong."

Rikki's eyes flooded with tears. "Back where I belong."

As one of those tears slid down Rikki's cheek, Quinn kissed it away, tasting the salt on his lips.

Were those tears for him? If she didn't think she belonged with him by now, he'd have to up his game to convince her otherwise. And he'd start tonight.

THE NEXT MORNING, Quinn pulled on a pair of cargo shorts with big side pockets as he watched Rikki tuck her gun into a purse.

"It's times like these I wish I had a purse." Quinn grabbed his own weapon and slipped it into a pocket of his shorts where it banged against his thigh. "I'd like to carry bigger, but I don't want to be obvious."

Rikki held up her purse, swinging it from her fingertips. "I'd like to carry bigger, too, but I'm not going to lug around a suitcase."

"Remember—" he took her by the shoulders, his thumb nestling beneath the strap of her purse "—stay out of sight, even when I get her alone. She doesn't need to know you're still alive."

"Got it."

"Nobody knows Rikki Taylor is alive. There's no reason for anyone to know April Thompson is alive, either, or Agent Reid, or whoever you were for Belinda's friends."

He released her, and she adjusted the straps of her sundress. Then she crossed to the bed and swept up a big hat. "I'll be wearing this for cover, too."

"Once I make contact with her and show her my gun, I'll walk her to the park in the opposite direction of the coffeehouse where you'll be waiting. Stay there until I text you or come and get you. I'll only come and get you when I'm sure Belinda is on her way home and can't see you."

"But if she still has the picture of David, you'll be going back home with her to get it, right?"

"I'm hoping for even better proof he's alive, so don't hold your breath on that picture."

"Just don't drink anything she offers."

"Don't worry about that."

They would be arriving to the area separately, so Quinn left first with the car. Rikki would be taking a taxi later. He didn't want her anywhere near Belinda Dawson after what Belinda had tried last night, but trying to keep Rikki away would take more patience than he had. Also, he'd discovered that keeping Rikki away was not in his DNA.

Quinn parked a few blocks away from the Savannah Historical Society and waited in his car for almost thirty minutes. They'd checked the volunteer shifts for that morning, and five minutes before he figured Belinda would be leaving, he walked to the block that housed the building and sat on a park bench facing the front entrance. She couldn't exit to the rear, and if she came out a side door, she'd be forced to this street anyway. He had it all sussed out—but the best-laid plans had a way of taking a twist.

He glanced casually to his right at the coffeehouse with its umbrellaed tables spilling onto the sidewalk, and his heart jumped when he spied a big white hat with a black-and-white polka-dot band around it— as long as she stayed out of sight.

Quinn shifted his focus back to the building that housed the Historical Society and his eyes narrowed as he picked out Belinda skipping down the two steps, her arm tucked around the arm of another woman.

Quinn shook his head. As far as Belinda knew, she'd poisoned a woman last night, and she looked like a sorority sister going to lunch.

He held his breath as he watched the two women. He hadn't planned on dealing with a second person.

When the other woman peeled off in another direction, Quinn let out his breath and pushed himself up from the bench. Go time.

Quinn ripped back the Velcro on his shorts' pocket and gripped his gun inside—not that he planned to use it, but he wouldn't mind putting a little fear into the woman who'd poisoned Rikki.

Belinda kept her eyes glued to her phone as she strode down the sidewalk.

Quinn moved behind her and quickened his pace. He lost the element of surprise as she swung her head around and then tripped to a stop.

"You."

He slowed his gait as he continued to approach her, his hand curled around the gun in his pocket. "You killed my partner, and I wanna know why. I wanna know where your husband is."

Belinda's eyes widened and she licked her lips, her gaze dropping to his pocket. "I-I…"

A zipping sound ripped through the air. Belinda's eyes bugged out of their sockets one second before she collapsed in front of him.

Chapter Fourteen

Rikki squinted through the small binoculars she cupped in the palm of her hand. As Belinda turned to confront Quinn, Rikki whispered, "Shoot. You gotta have more stealth than that, sailor."

Then Belinda's body jerked, and she fell to the ground.

With her heart pounding in her chest and a voice screaming in her head, Rikki jumped up from the table, knocking over her glass of water. Clutching her purse against her body, she ran across the street toward the Historical Society.

Her vision blurred as she ran, and she could no longer see Quinn standing on the sidewalk. She panted and bumped into someone running from the scene.

Someone shouted, "Active shooter."

Rikki jogged toward the downed figure and as she got close, a hand shot out from behind a tree and grabbed her.

Quinn pulled her back behind the tree with him. "Someone shot her. He might still be active. I don't think she's dead."

"I need to talk to her." She broke away from Quinn and dropped to the ground. Sirens wailed in the distance, and most people had hit the pavement or had taken cover behind trees.

Rikki crawled toward Belinda, her hand stretched out and her fingers curled. She grabbed Belinda's hand and scooted toward her, nose to nose.

Quinn had followed her and crouched beside her, blocking her from the direction of the sniper.

Blood seeped out from beneath Belinda's body, but her eyes were open and she'd zeroed in on Rikki's face. Her lips parted and she croaked.

Rikki squeezed her hand. "I need to know where David is."

Belinda gasped and mumbled, and Rikki put her ear close to her lips.

"Not telling you. Did you think I didn't know you when I saw you? David's beloved Rikki."

Rikki's mouth fell open.

"Wasn't sure. Then you saw picture. You knew. 'Course you knew David's body. You were his lover."

"That never happened. He turned on me. Set me up." Rikki rushed her words as the sirens from the ambulance sounded louder.

"Revenge, you broke it off. When I told him you were alive, it gave him…life." Belinda's lips twisted, whether in pain or bitterness, Rikki couldn't tell.

"So I wanted to take your life again. Away from him."

"Who did this to you? Where's David now?"

"Davey did it. You don't cross David."

An EMT's voice shouted above them. "Ma'am, ma'am. I need you to get out of the way now."

"Tell me. We'll take him down together." Rikki gripped Belinda's wrist. "Where is he?"

The EMT physically pulled Rikki away from Belinda, but not before she choked out one word. "Song."

Quinn took her arm, and his head swiveled back and forth like a weather vane in a hurricane. "You put yourself in extreme danger. Was it worth it?"

"Her last word to me? *Song.* Buddy Song knows where David is. I'd say that's worth it. The sniper was long gone anyway."

He cocked one eyebrow in her direction as he practically dragged her across the street. "Because you're an expert on snipers?"

"Well, he wasn't a very good one, was he? He didn't kill Belinda."

"Not yet."

"She seemed pretty lucid for someone on death's doorstep. She could very well recover from this."

"Maybe that sniper didn't want to kill her. Maybe he just wanted to interrupt her conversation with me or teach her a lesson about going rogue and murdering random CIA agents."

"Wasn't he ready to murder random CIA agents the other night at Belinda's house?"

"We don't know what his intentions were that night. He could've just wanted to trap and question, like I planned to do with Belinda." He took her hand and led her into a small public parking lot. "I'm in here."

She ducked into the car and slumped in the seat. "At least we can now start with Buddy Song."

"We knew about him anyway, and Belinda could've been lying." He cranked on the engine and squealed out of the parking lot. "What else was she telling you? That conversation lasted longer than one name."

"Oh, yeah." Rikki slumped farther in the seat. "She knew who I was."

"What?" Quinn stomped on the brakes at the stop sign, and her body strained against the shoulder strap and then thumped back.

"She made me." Rikki twisted her fingers in her lap. "She suspected who I was when we first got to her house, and when I showed interest in the picture, that confirmed it for her."

"Maybe she won't recover."

"Quinn." She jerked her head around.

"I'm supposed to be rooting for a woman who called out a gunman on us, tried to poison you and now knows your identity?" He lifted his shoulders. "I'm sorry. I don't have much sympathy for her. I don't want her blabbing to anyone in the CIA about you before we're ready, and we won't be ready until someone talks to Buddy Song or Chan decodes David's emails."

"It's too late." Rikki pressed her hands against her stomach. In the shock of Belinda's shooting and getting info about David out of her, Rikki hadn't dwelled on the fact that Belinda had known who she was from the get-go. Now the truth of it punched her in the gut.

"She already told someone, and it's the reason why she tried to kill me."

"Back up. Who'd she tell? Did that person order her to poison you?"

"She told David."

Quinn uttered an expletive. "And David ordered your death a second time? I can't wait to get my hands on him."

"I'm not sure it went down like that." Rikki dug her fingers in her hair. "Belinda told David I was alive, and apparently, he was a little too happy about it for Belinda's liking. She always thought David and I were lovers, and his reaction to her news seemed to confirm that for her."

Quinn's jaw tightened. "David lied to her, told her you came onto him. She told us as much."

"Probably." Rikki rolled her shoulders, but the stress just clawed its way up her neck. "His reaction to my being alive wasn't what she'd hoped for, so she decided to take me out—it sounds like to spite him."

He swung the car into a parking space at their motel and threw it into Park. "She thinks her own husband ordered this hit on her today because she tried to kill you? Does David really think you're going to forgive him for setting you up as a traitor?"

"I don't know what David thinks. It sounds like he's gone completely off the deep end, but it gave me a little leverage with her to give up some intel on David."

"Buddy Song's name is hardly intel. If David knows you're still alive, it won't be long before the CIA knows."

"He's not exactly going to call them from the dead, is he?"

"He'll use other methods to get the news out. You know he will." He stroked her arm from shoulder to wrist. "Do you want to take what we have now and go to the Agency? Do you want to turn yourself in?"

"Take what we have?" She snapped off her seat belt. "We have nothing. No proof. I don't even have that picture of David with the tattoo he never had before his supposed death."

Quinn lifted his hips from the seat of the car and dug into his voluminous pocket. He pulled out a cell phone and held it in front of her face. "I have this."

"Belinda's?" Her heart skipped in her chest and she pounced on the phone, snatching it from Quinn's hand.

"She was holding it when I approached her. When the bullet hit her, she dropped it and I scooped it up."

Rikki pressed the phone to her chest. "Quick thinking."

"Let's regroup and get your life back."

When they returned to the motel room, Rikki huddled in a chair by the window and tapped Belinda's phone to wake it up. "Ugh, it's password-protected."

"You know how to get around that, right? Isn't that CIA 101?"

"There are a couple of ways I can get in, although every time the manufacturers hear about another trick to bypass security codes, they change things up." Rikki tapped through several key sequences and let out a pent-up breath when Belinda's home screen popped up. "I'm in. This looks like her real phone and not the temp she used to call you."

"And which she probably used to contact her husband." Quinn circled his finger in the air. "She'll have her personal stuff on this one, though."

Rikki swept her finger through Belinda's photos. "Lots of pics of Savannah and her house. She must've done some remodeling lately."

"That's not gonna help."

"Wait." With a shaking finger, Rikki tapped an image of a shirtless man. "It's here. The picture of David with that tattoo that he never had before he died."

"All right!" Quinn pumped his fist in the air. "Now, who can verify that the tattoo is a new acquisition besides you?"

"Anyone who did PT with David. If they changed in the locker room with him or even if he wore a tank top during PT, his chest would've been on display, and I'm telling you he never had that giant phoenix tattoo."

"You're going to send that to Ariel." Quinn leveled a finger at the phone. "What's your answer if someone tries to claim he got it in Korea?"

"Not enough time—and look at it." She jabbed her finger at the serious face in the picture, the face she used to trust. "It's not a brand-new tattoo. We weren't in Korea long enough for something like that to heal up. Hell, we weren't in Korea long enough before we were captured for him to even get a tattoo like that. Don't those tattoo artists take several days to create a work of art like that?"

"It could take more than one sitting. It looks like we might have Dawson dead to rights on this." Quinn rubbed his chin and gazed over her right shoulder.

"What? I don't like that look."

His gaze snapped back to her face. "Dawson knows you're alive."

"Y-yes?" She squared Belinda's phone on the table and clasped her hands between her knees.

"He might try to get word to the CIA—anonymously, of course."

"Why would the Agency believe a man who faked his own death in North Korea and set up his partner to take the fall as a traitor?"

"What if he already beat us to the punch? What if the CIA already got a tip that Rikki Taylor is alive and well and skulking around Savannah, and is taking action?" Quinn paced to the window and back to the TV, his long stride eating up the space in a few steps.

Rikki's eyes wandered to the window of their dumpy motel and fixed on a road sign across the street. "You mean like right now?"

"We need to get out of this town and back to New Orleans." Quinn stopped in midturn. "Does Dawson know much about me? Where I live?"

"I never told him anything. He knew we were... together in Dubai, and he probably knew your name and knew that you were a SEAL from asking around, but I doubt if he got any personal info on you, and I certainly didn't tell him anything like that."

"Navy's not going to give him any details about me, but then he's CIA. He can get those details his own way."

Rikki shook her head. "I don't think he would've done that, and he can't do it now."

"Let's head back tonight." He grabbed the remote from the bed. "You up for an all-night drive?"

"To get out of Savannah? Hell, yeah."

Quinn clicked on the TV. "We don't even know if Belinda made it or not."

"I'm sure she did. From the blood pooling, it looked like she got hit in the back. Although she was losing a lot of blood, she was conscious and the EMTs got right to work on her."

Quinn flipped through the channels until he settled on some local news. "We may have missed the story. It must've been the lead."

"The hospital won't tell us anything." Rikki pushed herself up from the chair and stood in front of the TV with her arms crossed. Even though Belinda Dawson had tried to poison her, Rikki couldn't help feeling sorry for her. She must really love David to keep his secrets, secrets that could get her charged with espionage, and then to believe the man you loved, the man you'd protected, was obsessed with someone else must be torture.

Rikki had watched her mother bounce from man to man, putting her faith in love time after time only to have her heart broken. No man was worth that kind of pain.

Rikki's gaze slid to Quinn, perched on the foot of the bed, hunched forward. He was different from any man her mom had followed around the world. Sincere. Loyal. Family-oriented.

And he didn't know he had one.

His head jerked to the side. "What?"

"Just thinking about Belinda." Rikki gathered her hair into a ponytail. "When do we get out of here?"

"As soon as you can throw your stuff together. We can eat on the road."

"Have you heard anything more from Chan about David's emails?"

"Not yet. Did you send that picture of Dawson to your phone?"

As she reached for Belinda's phone on the table, Quinn said, "Wait. Better yet. Send that picture to my phone, and I'll send it along to Ariel. My phone is untraceable and won't come up on anyone's radar. We don't want that photo leaking out. Dawson's not going to know we have it, and we don't want to clue him in."

Rikki cupped Belinda's phone in her palm. "David knows I'm alive, but does he realize that I know he's alive?"

"I'm assuming Belinda told him, right?" He grabbed his phone and aimed it at her. "Send it."

"She didn't really say one way or the other. I guess if she told him about my seeing the picture, he'd know that I figured it out." She tapped the phone to text the picture to Quinn's number. "Why?"

"Just wondering if Dawson would try to contact you."

Heat prickled across her skin, and she dropped the phone. It clattered on the table. "Why would he?"

Quinn lifted one shoulder. "To make some kind of overture."

"Overture?" Rikki's eye twitched and she rubbed it. "What kind of overture could he make with me now after setting me up as a traitor to the CIA and arranging to have me killed? How do you start that conversation?"

He joined her at the table and rubbed her back. "I hope you don't have to find out."

"Let's get out of here." She held up Belinda's phone. "I'm taking this with me. Who knows what else I can discover on here?"

Quinn dragged his bag from the closet floor. "Any texts?"

"Just a couple with some girl talk." Rikki pocketed Belinda's phone. "I wonder what all of Belinda's good, good friends would think about her if they knew she ran around poisoning drinks and covering for her traitor husband."

"They're going to find out soon enough once we get this investigation in official hands. That woman's going to get hers for trying to kill you."

Rikki pressed her lips together as she started packing. Having Quinn on her side gave her a warm glow in her belly.

Quinn had given her something else in her belly eighteen months ago, and she planned to tell him all about that little miracle when they got back to New Orleans.

As THEY HEADED out of Savannah, Rikki dug Belinda's phone from her pocket. "I'm going to look through this while it's still working. Once Belinda realizes her phone is missing, she'll have it deactivated."

"We don't even know if she's dead or alive. The most recent report I saw on my phone was that someone had been critically injured in that shooting, nothing about a fatality."

"I think if she'd died it would've made the news. Nothing about a suspect?"

"He's not going to be caught, and if she survives, Belinda's not going to implicate anyone."

Rikki rolled back the seat and wedged her bare feet against the glove compartment. "Do you mind?"

"You can put your feet anywhere." Quinn reached forward and caressed her ankle.

She curled her toes and almost purred. Instead, she thumbed through Belinda's pictures. "No more suspicious photos. Either that's the only one David sent her, or she deleted the rest."

"We lucked out with that one."

"Yep." She squinted at the text messages as she scrolled through each set. "No new messages, either. It's creepy that there's a text here to one of her friends about drinks the other night. Funny she doesn't mention the poison."

"Yeah, that's just what you want to tell your old friends. Meeting for drinks, and by the way, don't mind the dead chick at the table."

Rikki tapped Belinda's contacts and swept her finger down the list. One name flew by, and she gasped.

"What?"

"One of her contacts." Rikki dragged her finger back up the names and stopped on the most important one. "Frederick Von."

"You're kidding." Quinn flexed his fingers on the wheel of the car. "Dawson should've trained his wife better in the rules of espionage."

"Who would know the name of David's villain in an unpublished work of fiction? Besides, I'm sure he believed Belinda would never come under suspicion, that *he'd* never come under suspicion."

"And yet here they are—under suspicion." Quinn cranked his head to the side. "What are you going to do about it?"

She held the phone between both of her hands as if in prayer. "You think I should call him?"

"I do."

"If I do, I'm going to play nice." She tapped her steepled fingers against her chin. "I'm going to pretend I don't know he set me up."

Quinn raised his eyebrows as he studied the road in front of him. "Do you think he's gonna believe that?"

"I'll make him believe it. Why would I think he set me up? I thought he'd been killed, I was captured by the North Koreans, and I don't know anything about the CIA trying to take me down as a traitor."

"Devil's advocate here." He tapped his chest. "If you don't know he set you up, why haven't you gone straight to the Agency? Why are you floundering around Louisiana and Georgia?"

She held up one finger. "I didn't say the CIA didn't think I was a traitor. I just don't know *why* they think I'm one."

"He's gonna be suspicious as to why you don't believe it's him. He faked his death, you were captured, there was no Vlad."

"I just *thought* he died and we were both played."

"Do you think he'll believe you?"

Rikki dipped her head to hide her warm cheeks behind a veil of hair. "I think I can make David Dawson believe anything if I put my mind to it."

The silence stretched between them, and Rikki peeked at Quinn's hard profile.

He cleared his throat. "Then do it."

She wiped the back of her hand across her forehead despite the air-conditioning blasting her face. With an unsteady finger, she tapped Frederick Von and then put the phone on Speaker, even though she really didn't want Quinn listening to this conversation.

The phone rang, and Rikki clutched the seat's armrest. It rang several more times before a pleasant recording told her the phone's owner didn't have voice mail set up.

Rikki snorted. "I'd like to hear that voice mail greeting."

"Try again later. We have no idea where he is or what time zone he's in." He hunched forward and rapped a knuckle against the windshield. "Let's stop for some food and knock out the rest of this trip."

Four hours later and halfway through the drive, Rikki poked through one of the bags from the fast-food restaurant they'd driven through for dinner. "Do you want the rest of these French fries?"

"Are you hungry again? We can stop. We're making good time."

"Not really." She stuffed one of the fries in her mouth and licked the salt from her fingers. "Just bored."

"Do you feel like driving?"

"Too tired."

"Take a nap."

Belinda's cell, which Rikki had tucked beneath her right thigh, buzzed to life. She grabbed the phone and felt the blood drain from her face. "It's him."

"Are you ready?" Quinn put on his signal to pull into a rest area.

Rikki licked her lips and nodded. "Hello?"

The man's voice, David's voice from the grave, started before the first word left Rikki's lips.

"Belinda, what the hell are you doing calling me on this phone? I don't care if you have me listed as Dr. Seuss. You don't use this phone, especially not now."

"David, it's Rikki."

He sucked in a breath across the miles. "Rikki? My God. It sounds like you. What was the name of the bartender our first night in Athens?"

"Gypsy Rose."

A noisy rush of air gushed over the line. "Wh-when Belinda told me you were alive, I couldn't believe it."

Rikki met Quinn's gaze and dipped her chin once. David would admit nothing, whether he thought she believed him or not. She could do this.

Squaring her shoulders, she pinned them against the seat back. "I felt the same way when I discovered you were alive."

"From the picture. You saw the picture. That's what Belinda said. You knew. You knew me so well, you could tell it was recent."

Quinn made a sharp movement in the driver's seat, and Rikki placed a hand on his thigh.

They'd have to both get through this. "It was the tattoo, David."

"Of course." He coughed. "What did Belinda tell you?"

"Tell me? She told me nothing, but I saw the picture."

"Who was the man with you when you came to the house?"

"A paid associate." She squeezed Quinn's knee. "He doesn't know anything about what I'm doing."

David paused for two beats. "What are you trying to do, Rikki? Why aren't you with the Agency... or are you?"

"As far as I can tell, the Agency thinks I'm a traitor. That debacle in North Korea pretty much torpedoed both of our careers." She paused herself. "Why aren't you with the Agency? Where are you?"

"Deep undercover. The Agency thinks I'm dead, and I want to keep it that way. But what happened to you? I'd heard from my guy in South Korea that you'd been killed."

David's voice actually broke, and Rikki had to grip the phone harder to keep from throwing it out the window.

"The North Koreans captured me."

"Oh my God. We both know what that means. How'd you escape?"

"I had some help and some good luck. Seems like we both did." For just a moment, the knots in Rikki's stomach had loosened and it felt like old times talking with David about an assignment.

She only had to glance at Quinn's tight jaw to remember it wasn't.

"What have you been doing, David? Where are you? What happened to your lead on Vlad? Was it all counterintelligence?"

"That's the thing, Rikki. I'm hot on Vlad's trail right now. This will be my ticket back to the Agency—mine and yours."

Quinn poked her in the ribs, but he didn't have to prod her to encourage David in this line of thinking.

"Your intel panned out?"

"Once I escaped from the North Koreans, I buckled down and burrowed in. I'm getting ready to bring down Vlad and I couldn't be happier that you're alive to help me do it." He cleared his throat. "Just like old times, Rikki, right? You want to do this with me, right?"

Quinn jabbed her again, and she didn't know if he approved or not, but Rikki refused to look at him—just in case he wanted to dissuade her.

"O-of course, David. I'm in."

"You sound hesitant. You believe me, don't you, Rikki? You believe I never meant our operation to go down like that—you captured, us split up."

"I… Yes."

"Of course things are a little different now, but we can work around all that."

"Different? You mean because we're rogue agents instead of official ones with support from the CIA?"

"There's that…and the other matter. Your personal issue."

Quinn jerked in the seat beside her, and Rikki's heart began to hammer painfully in her chest.

"My personal issue?"

"You know—the fact that you have a daughter now. You can't try to tell me that little redheaded baby in Jamaica with your mother isn't yours."

Chapter Fifteen

The roaring in Quinn's ears sounded like a Mack truck coming up behind them in the rest stop. His gaze flew to Rikki's face, a white oval in the darkness of the car.

Quinn waited for the eye roll. The laugh. The denial.

She stammered. "Wh-what are you talking about? You're in Jamaica?"

The bastard's voice lowered, silky smooth. "I'm not in this alone, Rikki. As soon as Belinda told me the good news that you were alive and well and…snooping around Savannah with a big bodyguard type, I sent one of my associates out to Jamaica. You see how well we know each other? I remembered your mother was out there. I thought maybe we could get some information about you out of her, and my associate discovered something even better."

The only response Rikki could muster was a small gurgle, and Quinn clenched his jaw so hard he thought his teeth would break.

No denial. It had to be true. A child? A baby?

Did it happen in Korea? Good God, it couldn't be David's.

David's voice continued, and Quinn just wanted to punch the phone.

"Don't try to deny she's yours, Rikki. I've only ever seen that hair color on one other person." Dawson's voice had an almost dreamy quality, and Quinn clenched his fists. "That, and we asked around. The locals are talkative, especially when cash is involved."

Rikki's lips emitted small bursts of air, as if she couldn't take in enough air to breathe. "Better?"

"What?"

"You said better. Why is discovering my...daughter better?"

Quinn wanted to shake Rikki, but she hadn't even looked at him since Dawson dropped the bombshell. Had she been raped in the labor camp? Quinn's blood boiled in his veins.

David sucked in a breath. "Having a child is a happy occasion, and she's not a small infant. Although I don't know much about babies, I do know yours must've been conceived before we left for Korea."

A shaft of pain pierced the back of Quinn's head. He wanted to grab the phone and end the call. He wanted Rikki to look at him. He wanted her to explain.

"Of course it's happy." Rikki leaned her head against the window. "I just don't understand your interest in my child."

"Everything about you interests me, Rikki. Let's just say, I need your help on this Vlad assignment. I've always needed you, Rikki."

"I'll help you. Where are you?"

"We'll talk again later…partner."

"D-don't you want to hear about Belinda? How I happen to have her phone?"

"I don't really care. Just keep it."

Quinn had been building to the boiling point during that call and wanted to pounce on Rikki with a million questions and accusations. But when Dawson ended the call, he sat there, staring out the window at the Alabama trees guarding the rest area, feeling like he'd been steamrollered.

Rikki didn't move, but mewling noises started coming from the other side of the car where she was huddled against the window.

Quinn opened his mouth, but he couldn't form any words, would probably sound like Rikki right now.

He swallowed and tried again. "What's going on? Whose baby?"

Rikki sniffled, and Belinda's phone slid from her hand and dropped to the floor of the car. "She's yours, Quinn. Ours."

Quinn covered his face with his hands. He had a baby with Rikki. How did she manage to keep it from him all this time? She lied for a living.

Cool fingers encircled his wrist. "I'm sorry. I was going to tell you. I'd planned to tell you all along, but—" she waved one arm in the small confines of the car "—this all got in the way."

Rikki's voice had a tone he'd never heard from her before—pleading, unsure, frightened—and it shocked him out of his trance.

He dropped his hands from his face and rounded on her, grabbing her shoulder. "You were pregnant before you were in Korea."

"Y-yes. Of course. Bella is yours."

"Oh God, Rikki." He cupped the side of her face, his thumb caressing her wet cheek. "You were pregnant while you were in that labor camp."

She dropped her lashes, sticky with her tears. "I was."

"You must've been terrified, not only for yourself but for the baby."

"I just assumed I was going to lose her, and even after I escaped, I was concerned she might suffer."

A fist squeezed Quinn's heart and his breath caught in his throat. "Did she? Is she…?"

Rikki met his eyes for the first time, and a soft smile hovered on her lips. "Oh, Quinn. She's perfect in every way. You understand, don't you? You do understand why I had to keep her a secret, even from you?"

"I'm sure it didn't help my case for fatherhood when you found out I was the one behind that sniper rifle."

Her eyes widened, and fresh tears began a path down her face. "But she's not a secret anymore. David knows. He has someone in Jamaica."

"He's not going to do anything." He threaded his fingers through Rikki's hair and pulled her in for a quick kiss. "The guy still loves you."

She choked. "He set me up to be killed or captured, ruined my career, and just threatened my daughter. That's love?"

"The twisted, obsessive, delusional kind." He took both her hands in his. "The kind that you can use. You're not above using David Dawson, are you?"

"Who, me?" She lifted her shoulder and wiped her nose on her sleeve. "Hell no."

Quinn chuckled. "That's my Rikki Taylor. Now you've got another four hours on the road to tell me all about our daughter, Bella, but first you need to call your mother in Jamaica and give her a heads-up. Do she and your stepfather have people they can trust out there? People to look after them?"

"Oh, yeah. Chaz, my stepfather, has been down there for years. The locals have adopted him, adopted Bella."

"Good. She needs everyone looking out for her." He reached into his front pocket and pulled out his phone. "Use this one. Will your mom be alarmed?"

"My mom is accustomed to my work, and Chaz will make sure she stays calm. She takes all her cues from him."

"That's a good thing right now."

As Quinn got back on the road, he half listened as Rikki explained to her mother the need to keep Bella safe.

She ended the call and heaved a sigh. "Mom had

already noticed a couple of tourists eyeing Bella at the hotel."

"Maybe you got the spy gene from your mom. Did you scare her?"

"A little, but she got Chaz right on the phone and he assured me they'd take care of Bella. I trust him… and the locals."

Quinn rolled his shoulders. "When did you find out you were pregnant?"

Rikki's posture stiffened. "I swear, Quinn. I had no idea until I was in South Korea. I thought the food didn't agree with me."

"You don't have to defend your decisions, Rikki."

"Why not? I figured the longer I waited to tell you, the more furious you'd be with me for keeping it from you, and now…you don't seem furious at all."

"What right do I have to be mad? When were you supposed to tell me? The moment you discovered it was me on the other end of that sniper rifle waiting and willing to take you down?"

"You didn't."

"You've been through hell and back, Rikki, keeping our daughter safe through it all. I owe you nothing but gratitude. But you know what this means, right?"

She folded her hands and clasped them between her knees. "What?"

"You're never leaving me high and dry again."

"I don't want to, Quinn, ever."

He might be a fool, but he believed her.

"Now tell me all about our daughter."

BY THE TIME they reached New Orleans, Quinn had already carved out a place in his heart for his little Bella, a girl with her mother's ginger curls and her father's stubbornness, although he secretly thought that trait came from Mom, too.

As Quinn inserted his key in the lock of his front door, Rikki put her hand over his. "Do you think your place could've been compromised?"

"Dawson wouldn't be able to get any information on me."

Rikki chewed on her bottom lip. "I don't know. He found out your name in Dubai and knew you were a navy SEAL."

"Navy's not going to give him anything." He held up his hand. "And before you tell me Dawson's some kind of CIA superagent, the CIA isn't going to give him anything, either."

He studied Rikki's face—eyebrows drawn over her nose, lips twisted into a frown—and pulled out his weapon. "Stay back."

He pushed open his front door and swept his gun from side to side as he scanned the living room and kitchen. "Everything looks in order."

Following him over the threshold, Rikki took out her own weapon and crouched behind him as he moved toward the back of the apartment. They searched through both of the rooms and found nothing out of place.

Quinn double-locked his front door. "Feel better?"

Rikki sagged against the doorjamb of the bedroom. "Not really. David knows about you. He must know Bella is yours, and maybe he even figured out you paid a visit to Belinda with me."

"Then it's your job—" he touched Rikki's nose with the tip of his finger "—to convince him he's the only man in your life."

"He's not a fool, Quinn."

"When a man has feelings about a woman like Dawson has about you, he'll be only too eager to believe what you're puttin' down."

She quirked an eyebrow at him. "Speaking from experience?"

"One of many differences between me and Dawson." Quinn held up a finger. "I'm in love with you, not obsessed with you. That allows me to look at you realistically. That's why I let you go when you hightailed it out of Dubai and left me holding the sheets. For whatever reason, you couldn't handle the feelings between us. It cut me to the core, but you had to do what worked for you. If you could figure it out and come back to me, I would be there with open arms."

"I figured it out, sailor." She wrapped her arms around his waist and rested her head against his chest.

He stroked her hair. "Dawson doesn't want to let you go. He pissed off his own wife, the woman keeping his secrets, with his reaction to the news that you weren't dead. Then he probably tried to have her killed for attempting to poison you."

"We don't know if that was David behind the

shooting. He answered that phone call from me as if he thought it was Belinda."

"Maybe the order was to shoot his wife, but not to kill her. When he saw the call from her cell, of course he'd act like he didn't know anything about the attempt on her life."

"That's so cold."

"He doesn't want Belinda. He wants you, Rikki, and you're going to give him what he wants." He squeezed the back of her neck. "Are you okay with that? We can do it a different way—bring in Dawson and find out his connection with Vlad."

"If you think I'm going to let this opportunity pass me by, there are a few more things I need to teach you about myself before you start professing your love for me again."

"I'm sure there are a lot of things you can still teach me about yourself, but none of that's going to change how I feel." He wrapped her in a bear hug and rested his chin on top of her head.

She spoke into his chest. "And I'm ready to give David what he wants."

Quinn tightened his hold on her. "But first you're gonna give me what I want."

"Always, Quinn McBride."

He swept her up in his arms to carry her to his bedroom, but his lust couldn't blot out the twinge of uneasiness in his heart.

She still hadn't told him she loved him. He wanted

more than her body. He wanted more than Bella to bind them together.

He wanted her love, unconditional and unreserved.

THE FOLLOWING MORNING, they worked on a plan over breakfast.

Quinn stabbed a clump of scrambled eggs and shook it at Rikki. "Dawson wants to bring you into his scheme. He always wanted that. Whether he believes you're game because he has someone watching Bella or because you've realized you can't live without him, doesn't matter. But he'll be more open with you if he believes the latter."

"I think I can pull it off, but if he knows I'm with you, that's going to put a serious crimp in my game. He was so jealous of you."

Quinn squirted some ketchup on his plate. "You've got an ace in the hole."

"I do?"

"I was the sniper who tried to take you out. Everyone believes I did the job. Dawson has to know that." He swept a forkful of eggs through the ketchup and held it over his plate as a red drop fell into the pile of eggs. "How could a woman ever forgive that, even if the sniper is the father of her baby?"

Hunching forward, Rikki broke a piece of toast in two. "That's believable. I can make a story out of that."

"Make that case to Dawson. And you need to tell Ariel what's going down."

"I will. Maybe she can send reinforcements for whatever David has planned."

"I forgot to mention." Quinn wiped his hands on a napkin and pulled his phone toward him with one finger. "Chan is making progress on Dawson's emails to Frederick Von, thinks he found a pattern, one he can enter into his computer program."

"The more evidence I can present to Ariel, the better. I'll let her take it to the CIA. I'm not going to the Agency directly."

"Good idea." Quinn stacked his plate on top of Rikki's. "Does Belinda's cell phone still work?"

"It does. She doesn't realize yet that it's missing, she's too injured to care or…she's dead."

Quinn tapped his phone. "Latest story I could find on the incident still lists one critically injured, no fatalities. Unless the CIA is hiding her condition from the press, it looks like she survived."

"Then David wanted her to survive."

"If it was David who ordered the hit." Quinn took their dishes to the sink. "I hope he plans to contact you soon, before Belinda turns that phone off."

"I did write down the number for Von, so I can always contact him if he doesn't get back to me."

"Yeah, but we want him reaching out to you first. He needs to make the first move." Quinn ran some water over the dishes and it hit him all over again that he was a father. He grinned. "When do I get to see some pictures of my little girl?"

"As soon as we get past this and we know Bella is safe, I'll have Mom text me some pictures to my temp phone."

"I can't wait." Quinn crossed the room to yank

open the drapes. "I'm picturing those red curls and big blue eyes just like her—"

Rikki screamed, "Get down!"

Instinct had him dropping his head and jerking to the side. He hit the floor—but not before he felt the searing pain of the bullet slam into his body. And all this time he'd thought he was bulletproof.

Chapter Sixteen

Her heart thundering in her chest, Rikki crawled toward Quinn bleeding on the floor. "Please, God. Please, God."

When she reached him, he groaned and spit out an expletive.

"Quinn, you're hit." She cupped his head with both hands, her fingers searching every inch of his scalp.

"It's not my head, damn it. It's my shoulder."

Quinn lay on his side, his knees to his chest, blood pooling beneath him.

"Thank God."

"Really? Because it hurts like hell."

A laugh bubbled to her lips, and she kissed the side of his intact head. "I thought… I thought, when I saw the blood… I thought…"

He rolled to his back with a low moan. "You need to come back to planet earth and tell me what it looks like."

She ripped off what was left of his shredded,

blood-soaked sleeve and peered at the damaged flesh. "Hang on. This is going to hurt."

She probed the wound and tucked her hand beneath his shoulder. "Went clean through, Quinn. Stay right here. I'll get some towels to stop the bleeding."

He grabbed her ankle as she started to crawl away. "No 911. We'll handle this."

Cranking her head over her shoulder, she said, "No 911, but you're going to have to see a doctor at some point. You need that properly cleaned, maybe some stitches, and you'll need some antibiotics for infection."

"I have some old antibiotics in the bathroom and ibuprofen. I need something to dull this pain."

Rikki didn't stand upright until she got to his hallway, away from that window. David. It had to have been David. They had both underestimated David's obsession with her. While still in good standing with the CIA, David had probably gotten a complete dossier on Quinn McBride once he learned about her affair with him.

She gathered several towels, wet down a few of them, and then snatched bottles of ibuprofen and expired antibiotics from a drawer in the bathroom.

She crawled back into the living room, pushing her medical supplies ahead of her. A few feet away from Quinn, she came to a dead halt and gagged.

He peeled open one eye where it gleamed from his bloody face. "Does it look bad?"

"What did you do? What happened? Why is that blood all over your face?"

"Because I'm a dead man. I just got shot in the head and you're going to take a picture of me for proof."

"For David."

"That's right. That bullet was meant for me, to get me out of the picture and out of your life."

"Why am I not crazy with grief?"

He scooped a little more blood from his shoulder wound and dragged it through his hair. "Because I'm the sniper the navy and the CIA sent to take you out. You always knew that. You were using me to get information and to help protect you against the CIA. Now you have Dawson."

Rikki left the towels and bottles on the floor and scooted toward the kitchen to retrieve her phone. She yanked on the charger to bring down her phone and made her way back to Quinn.

He positioned himself to resemble a man who'd been shot in the head, and as a navy SEAL sniper with plenty of kills under his belt, he knew exactly what that would look like.

"Take the pictures."

Rikki swallowed, almost believing the proof before her eyes and imagining how destroyed she would've been if the sniper had hit his mark.

She loved this man. He hadn't even been angry that she'd kept Bella's existence from him. His only concern had been how she'd begun her pregnancy in a North Korean labor camp and its effects on their baby.

She could give herself completely to Quinn and

he'd never use or abuse her devotion. He'd only return it tenfold.

She clicked several pictures of him and his bloody head, and then grabbed the towels.

Quinn rolled to his stomach. "Not yet. Get back on that phone and call Dawson. He'll expect it, either way. His guy is probably still watching the apartment building. He's gonna wonder where the lights and sirens are."

"David would know I'm not in any position to talk to the police and then the navy."

"Whatever. You need to make contact now. What reason would you have to keep silent, other than a desire to hide from him and hide the fact that his mission failed?"

"I hate him."

"Use that passion." He wiped his hand across his bloody mouth. "And hand me a towel so I can stop gushing blood on the floor."

She threw him a wet towel and a dry towel. "Bunch that dry towel under your shoulder and get on your back to apply pressure."

Taking a deep breath, she grabbed her phone and tapped the number she'd saved for David.

He must've been waiting, because he picked up on the first ring. "Yes?"

"It's Rikki."

"I figured as much. You okay?"

"Oh, I'm just fine, but Quinn McBride is dead, shot in the head right through his window. Are you crazy?" Her fingers got busy texting him Quinn's death shots.

"Do you care that much about him? The father of your baby? I could tell you a thing or two about your heroic Quinn McBride."

"Nothing I don't already know, like he was the navy SEAL sniper sent to eliminate me, the traitor."

David choked. "You knew that already?"

"Why do you think I came to see him right out of Jamaica? I wanted to take care of business. You taught me that, David."

Rikki glanced at Quinn, who'd paused from stanching his blood flow to stick his finger in his mouth. She scowled at him.

"But you didn't take care of business. You stayed with him, took him with you to visit Belinda."

"I needed him as a protector. He's all muscle and brawn, but not too much brain."

Quinn kicked her foot, and she stuck out her tongue at him.

"I knew the two of you weren't meant for each other, Rikki. I'm sorry I had him taken out right in front of you, but he has to be out of the picture for us to move forward."

"Oh, he's out of the picture." She tapped her phone several times and sent the last of Quinn's death pictures to David. "Am I safe now?"

"The sniper? He's long gone." David clicked his tongue. "Got the pictures. Once he saw McBride fall, he disassembled and took off—just in case you went ballistic and called in the authorities."

Rikki snorted. "No chance of that. Do you think I want to talk to a bunch of cops? Once they found out Quinn's identity, they'd call in the navy. No, thanks. His death needs to remain a secret for as long as possible."

"Any chance of discovery there?"

"Nobody heard the shot. There's a bullet hole in the window, but the velocity of the bullet was such that the window didn't shatter. McBride's deploying in another few weeks, and I'm assuming that's when his body will be discovered. He has no family to speak of. Nobody's going to miss him."

Quinn kicked her again.

"Good. There's someone very important I want you to meet. Plenty of people have already switched to his side. He pays well and he's loyal—unlike the Agency."

"Y-you don't mean who I think you mean, do you? I thought we were going out to Korea to provide information that would lead to his capture. Can't we still do that?"

"There's no need for it, Rikki. What he does is no different from what we were doing, but he's supporting different countries than we are. That's all. He's not interested in taking down the US, but he wants us to think twice before sticking our noses in other countries' business—countries he wants to control."

"I'm not saying I'm in, David, but I also won't betray you. I'm done with the Agency. Y-you were always my first loyalty anyway."

"We could do this together, Rikki—partners. I

could provide your daughter riches beyond belief, and with those riches, safety and security."

Rikki pressed a hand to her chest. Hearing David talk about her daughter struck fear in her heart. His threats against Bella always simmered beneath the surface. "When is this meeting? Where are you, David?"

"I'm where it all began for him, Rikki. I'm in Berlin."

Her gaze flew to Quinn's face, and he lifted his good shoulder.

"You want me in Berlin?"

"You must have an ID that you're using or you never would've made it to the US from Jamaica undetected. Besides, nobody knows you're alive except me and Belinda. We don't have to worry about McBride anymore."

"What about Belinda? Did you have her…shot?"

"I did. I had no intention of killing her, or she'd be dead." David made a strange hissing sound before speaking again. "I found out she tried to kill you, Rikki. She knew I was always in love with you. I couldn't allow that to stand. I wanted to let her know I could get to her anytime, anywhere. And now that you and I are going to be together, we don't have to give her another thought."

Rikki rubbed the sick feeling in her stomach. "Who is he? Who is Vlad?"

"You'll see."

David spent the rest of the phone call giving her

instructions for getting to Berlin, but wouldn't give her the meeting place with Vlad.

After his precise orders, David's voice softened. "I know you don't love me...yet. I know you're not on board with joining forces with the other side...yet. But I think you're halfway there on both, aren't you?"

"I think I've always been half in love with you, David." She glanced at Quinn, but he avoided her gaze in favor of tending to his wound. "The other... I don't know."

"I knew it, but I hope you understand, Rikki."

"Understand what?"

"If you don't join forces with our friend and do a really, really good job of pretending you love me, we'll take your daughter."

Chapter Seventeen

A white-hot fury coursed through Quinn's veins. His head felt light. Two seconds later, Rikki's cool hand fluttered about his face.

"You passed out." She folded a clean towel and applied pressure against his gunshot wound. "Enough of this nonsense. You need a doctor."

Quinn blinked and squeezed his eyes. "I need to find out where David is taking you to meet Vlad. This is our chance, maybe our one and only chance."

"You heard David. He's not going to tell me in advance. He's meeting me at the airport and taking me directly to the meeting. If he gets a hint that anyone has come with me or is following us, it's over, and it could be over for Bella. I'm not going to risk that."

"I'm not either." He winced as Rikki got aggressive with the pressure. "Following you is not good enough. We need to know the meeting place in advance so that we can set up."

Once she secured the towel against his arm and finished cleaning up his blood, Rikki scrambled to her feet and closed the drapes over the glass with the bullet hole.

"Let's get you up." She took his arm and helped him up.

He collapsed on the sofa, clutching the pill bottles in his hand. "Can you get me some water to down these?"

She took away the bloody towels and stuffed them into plastic garbage bags. She banged through his cupboards and returned with a bottle of water and a bottle of whiskey.

"Now that's a good idea, even at ten in the morning."

She shook the water bottle. "This first and then a shot of whiskey just so you won't pass out on me again."

"Yes, ma'am."

She twisted off the water bottle cap and handed the bottle to him.

He downed a couple of antibiotics and three ibuprofens. "You need to call Ariel now."

Rikki poured him a shot in a juice glass and thrust it at him. "Drink this first."

"You don't have to twist my arm." He threw back the whiskey, and the burning down his throat made his eyes water but cleared his senses. "Ariel."

Rikki got through to the head of the Vlad task force almost immediately, and Ariel's smooth voice almost purred over the line. "What do you have for me, Rikki?"

"Quinn McBride is listening in."

"I would expect that. Did David reach out to you?"

"You could say that. David hired someone to take out Quinn."

"Since Quinn's listening in on this call, I'm guessing the hit wasn't successful."

"Only because Rikki saw the laser and saved my life." Quinn laced his fingers through Rikki's. "Did I ever thank you for that?"

"You were in shock. I don't hold it against you."

Ariel sighed. "If you two are finished with your cute banter, what's the upshot?"

Rikki explained to Ariel how they faked Quinn's death and told her about David's proposal.

The pause from Ariel dragged on so long, Quinn exchanged a glance with Rikki. He thought Ariel would be all over this.

Finally she spoke, her voice strained and thin. "You're meeting with Vlad?"

"I am. I have to go through with it."

"And we need to be there to make sure it's the last meeting he ever has."

"Agreed." Quinn squeezed Rikki's hand before releasing her. "David Dawson is never going to fall for any surveillance. We have to know in advance and we have to be ready."

"It's yours, Quinn, yours and your teammates', all of them. I'm calling them all into Berlin right now, today."

Patting his shoulder, Quinn winced. "I'm not sure how much use I'm going to be with a sniper rifle right now. That shooter missed my head, but a bullet went clean through my shoulder."

"We have five other sniper rifles to back you up."

"Wait, wait." Rikki waved her hands in the air. "This all sounds wonderful, but we can't have six navy SEAL snipers roaming around Berlin looking for a meeting place."

Quinn rubbed his knuckles down Rikki's thigh. "I've been thinking about this. We have Dawson's phone number, Ariel."

"That's a start."

Rikki threw up another roadblock. "If you think you're going to put a trace on David's phone, he'll be way ahead of you. He's not going to take it with him."

Ariel said, "No, but he'll need to communicate with Vlad, and we can track those communications."

No wonder Ariel was leading this task force. Quinn snapped his fingers. "Exactly."

"Again." Rikki pushed the hair from her face and scooted to the edge of the sofa as if ready to do battle. "David and Vlad are not going to communicate in plain English or any other plain language."

"They'll use code." Quinn tapped her knee. "Like the code in those emails."

Ariel spoke up. "We're working on those."

"Ariel, I have a guy working them as well, and he's getting close."

"Berlin, huh?" Ariel's voice had a dreamy, faraway quality and Quinn raised his eyebrows at Rikki, who shrugged.

"I know Berlin is a big city, but this meeting won't

be in a public place. Vlad would be too worried about plants among the crowd."

"The forest." Ariel's voice rose with excitement. "The Grunewald forest is in Berlin."

Rikki scrunched up her nose. "I suppose that would be a good place for him. They would notice any people wandering around, wouldn't they? I know there are some schlosses there that attract tourists, but it's a big forest. Why did that come to mind, Ariel?"

She coughed. "Seems like it would work for him, but we need to do our research. When do you leave, Rikki?"

"I have a flight out tomorrow, and the meeting is the following day."

"That's not much time, but I can get Quinn's sniper team into Berlin tonight. I think Alexei Ivanov is still in LA. Miguel Estrada is in San Diego at Coronado. Josh Elliott is already back in Europe, as is Slade Gallagher, and Austin Foley is in the Middle East. I'll get them moving today, military transport."

"Whew." Quinn raised his eyes to the ceiling. "You're way ahead of me."

Ariel cut him off. "The number. Rikki, give me Dawson's number. We have to start intercepting now and hope we're not already too late."

When they finished their plans with Ariel and ended the call, Quinn drummed his fingers on the coffee table. "She's a dynamo for sure. Why is she so invested in bringing down Vlad, and what made her think of the Grunewald forest?"

"It's her job." Rikki bounded up from the sofa.

"I'm going to check in with Mom, and then I'm going to pack. You'd better start thinking about a disguise to get out of this apartment house in case it's being watched."

"Don't worry about me. I have a way out of here, and nobody ever has to know I left." He reached for his phone. "I need to get on Chan and tell him to expedite the decoding."

After sending a message to Chan, Quinn got on his own laptop and brought up Dawson's email exchanges with Vlad—he had to have been communicating with Vlad and Dawson had childishly given Vlad his own villain's name from his book. Hubris was one quality that usually brought people down, and Dawson was no different. He couldn't really believe that Rikki would fall in love with him, and yet here he was, making plans.

A sudden, piercing pain gripped Quinn's shoulder, and he grabbed it. He hoped he wasn't suffering from the same delusions as David Dawson.

Rikki charged in from the back rooms. "Bella's doing fine. Mom says there's a twenty-four-hour watch on their place by some tough dudes from Montego Bay. Nobody's going to get to her." She held up her phone. "And I just got off the phone with Ariel again. She's sending a doc around for a house call. I have his number. Maybe you can sneak him in."

"Better yet. We're sneaking out of here, or at least I am. You go out the regular way in case someone's watching my place."

"Where are we going?"

"I have a buddy who manages a hotel just off Rue

Royale. I did him a…favor once and he lets me have a suite at the hotel whenever I want."

"The Fourth of July weekend is coming up. Is he going to have anything available?"

"He usually has a high-end suite up for grabs that they use for upgrades. I'm calling in my chips."

TWO HOURS LATER, Quinn had sneaked out of his apartment through the basement and into a penthouse suite overlooking the French Quarter, and Rikki had followed him out the front door of his apartment and assured him nobody had followed her.

She stood next to him on the balcony, resting her head against his good shoulder. "This is going to work, Quinn."

"I have a backup plan in case we can't get your location in advance."

She folded her arms on the railing of the balcony and bent forward, surveying the street. "Shoot—or maybe I shouldn't be telling a sniper to shoot."

His lips twisted as he pointed to his bum shoulder. "I don't know when I'll be able to hoist my rifle again."

"There will be five other ones there to do the job, but what's the backup?"

"You're CIA, or you were. You must know about the internal GPS."

She dipped her head. "You mean the one that's swallowed?"

"That's the one. It's undetectable if they scan and search you, but we'll have your location."

"I can do that. I will do that, but it might be too

late once I'm there. Vlad probably has lookouts. Hell, he's a sniper himself, isn't he?"

"That's the problem, but it's better than nothing. Even if we miss Vlad, we might be able to go in and get Dawson."

"Don't miss Vlad." She dug her fingernails into his arm. "Whatever you do, whatever happens to me, don't let Vlad get away."

He cradled her jaw in his palm. "Do you think nailing Vlad is more important to me than you are? I'm not risking your life to get Vlad—and I'm not going to let anyone else do it, either."

She turned her head to kiss his hand. "You know we'll never be safe as long as he's alive. He has a personal vendetta against you guys. That's probably how David knew where you lived in New Orleans. Vlad may be distracted now because you've disrupted his plans so many times, but he'll come back at you and the others again and again."

"Let him." Quinn spread out his arms and faced the Mississippi, feeling invincible—until an ache claimed his shoulder.

"It's not just you, tough guy." She traced the outline of his bandage. "You have Bella now. You told me Miguel has a little boy, and Josh's girlfriend has a son. Austin Foley's girlfriend is not going to live on his parents' ranch forever, and Slade's new love puts herself in danger all over the world. And if you think that crazy, intense Russian, Alexei Ivanov is ever going to give up on Vlad, you're as crazy as he is. It has to end now—in Berlin, where according to David it all started for Vlad."

"Point taken. I shouldn't have updated you on all my teammates." Quinn scratched his jaw. "Dawson did say that, didn't he?"

"What?"

"That it all began in Berlin for Vlad."

"Y-yes." She dropped her lashes and shifted away from him.

"I'd heard that when Ariel was with the CIA, she spent time in Berlin."

"I think so." Rikki pointed across the rooftops to the river. "Are those barges always there?"

"Not usually. They're getting ready for the fireworks." He cocked his head at her, and she pushed herself off the balcony and spun around to the room.

"The doctor should be here soon."

Quinn wiped a bead of sweat from his forehead and followed her back into the air-conditioned room.

Ten minutes later the doc showed up, and he must've come from Ariel's special list, but Rikki still made herself scarce.

Dr. Smith, as he called himself, peeled back the homemade bandage from Quinn's shoulder and slipped his glasses to the edge of his nose. "Clean gunshot wound right there. You're lucky."

With very little further conversation, the doctor thoroughly cleaned the wound, replaced the bandage with something more secure, and gave Quinn a new bottle of antibiotics and some painkillers.

Dr. Smith shook the bottle of painkillers. "These

will make you sleepy, so you might want to stick with the ibuprofen."

Quinn picked up a sling and dangled it from his fingertips. "And this?"

"You'll want to hold your arm still and pressed against your body. That will help, but your shoulder is going to be stiff as hell if it isn't already."

Quinn rolled his shoulder back in a test and winced. "It's getting there."

"That's all I got for you." The doc snapped his black medical bag closed. "Take the antibiotics as prescribed. In the unlikely event the wound starts to fester, you'll need additional treatment. If you're still here, that'll probably be me, but I have a feeling—" Dr. Smith shot a glance at Rikki's bag in the corner "—you won't be here much longer."

Quinn got up and extended his hand. "I hope you mean I won't be in New Orleans much longer and not on this Earth."

The doctor chuckled. "With you guys, it's always a crapshoot."

When Dr. Smith left, Rikki sauntered in from the back bedroom. "Everything okay? You gonna live?"

"According to the cheerful doctor Ariel sent, that's debatable."

"What?" Rikki flew to his side and grabbed his hand.

"I'm kidding. He was referring to something other than the bullet hole in my shoulder. That's going to be just fine." He kissed the inside of her wrist. "How about you? Are you just fine with all this?"

"I've been fine with all this for almost ten years. It's my job, Quinn. I can handle David Dawson *and* Vlad."

"The stakes have never been higher, Rikki. You never had this much to lose—Bella."

"You." She brushed her knuckles across his cheek. "We're going to do this, Quinn. And then I'll introduce you to your daughter."

He squeezed the top of his shoulder. "I'm not sure I can do anything with this shoulder. How am I going to fire my rifle?"

"Your whole team will be there. It doesn't have to be you who takes out Vlad."

"After what we've been through with him, it would be a gold star for any of us. It might not just be Vlad. We might have to take down Dawson, too, although Ariel might prefer we bring him in for interrogation. Are you okay with that?"

"David is already dead to me. He turned, and he didn't even do it for ideology. He did it for money."

"And because he could—pride." Quinn toyed with the edge of his bandage. "You said you read his book, right?"

"Yeah, the whole thing." She rolled her eyes. "It was painful, and that was when I still liked the guy."

"Do you have it somewhere so I can read it?"

"You're not going to pick up any tips from it."

"Maybe not about writing, but there could be lots of tips about Dawson in there."

"I can get you to it." She stepped away from him and sat at the table with his laptop in front of her. "He put it up on a document-sharing platform for me to read. It's over a year old. I read it before we went to Dubai, so if he's made any changes they won't be in this draft."

"That's okay. Bring it up for me. I'll need something to read on my flight to Berlin. My military transport is not going to be as comfortable as your first class on a commercial airline."

Rikki spent several minutes at his laptop navigating to the shared document site. She scribbled something on a slip of hotel stationery and propped it up on his laptop's keyboard. "Here's my user name and password for this site."

Quinn stretched his arms over his head. "I'd better get packing. I leave tonight."

Rikki rose from the desk and returned to his side. She skimmed her hand down the front of his body and curled her fingers into the waistband of his shorts. "You didn't take any of those painkillers, did you?"

"No." When she touched him like that, he felt no pain at all.

"Because if you're leaving tonight, that means I have to spend the night in this giant suite in that giant bed all by myself."

His breathing grew shallow, and prickles of desire raced across his skin. "That would be a damned waste."

Sliding his hands down her back, he slanted his mouth across hers and kissed her hard and possessively. If she had to pretend to love Dawson, he didn't want her to forget what true love felt like.

She took his hand and led him into the suite's master bedroom.

Sometime later, with their legs and arms entwined around each other, when he didn't know where he ended and Rikki began, she kissed the edge of his jaw.

"I want you to know, Quinn McBride, before we go into this battle and risk everything, I love you. I loved you in Dubai. I loved you when I found out you'd had orders to kill me. I loved you when I found you again in New Orleans. And I love you now. I'm not afraid of love anymore, not your love."

He smoothed her hair back from her face. "That's all I ever wanted to hear from you."

Later that night, Dawson's words bounced on the screen as the C-5 hit an air pocket over the Atlantic. Quinn steadied his laptop.

The story dragged and Dawson's prose reeked, but Quinn couldn't shake the feeling that if Dawson used his villain's name for Vlad, there might be other hints in his work of fiction. Dawson must've been working with Vlad already when he penned this mess. In fact, Frederick Von seemed to be a thinly veiled reincarnation of Vlad.

Quinn plowed through the rest of the book, his eyelids drooping until a passage gave him a shot of adrenaline, a passage about Von's hideaway—a schloss in the Grunewald forest outside Berlin.

Chapter Eighteen

Ariel's team had a full day to set up at Grunewald before Rikki's meeting with Dawson and Vlad. They'd located a schloss in the forest owned by a blind trust.

In case Vlad had his people in the area, the sniper team came in as construction workers, tourists and locals out for a stroll. But if Vlad's people were counting, they'd know not everyone who'd entered the area for work or play left.

That first night with his brothers, his sniper team, had been like a homecoming for Quinn. They'd been scattered for so long, but the teamwork and comradery returned like second nature.

Alexei stroked his rifle like he would a beautiful woman. "Who's going to get the final shot at Vlad?"

"If there is a final shot." Austin Foley, gung ho and still a little green, looked up from his laptop. "We don't even know if this is the place."

"It's the place." Quinn formed his fingers into a gun and aimed at Austin.

Austin tapped the keyboard. "Rikki's in the hotel.

Are you sure Dawson won't be able to detect the GPS in her system?"

Slade Gallagher waved him off. "You worry too much, Austin. Dawson's not going to know, and if he suspects, he'll be confident that Vlad's people are not going to allow anyone to follow him and Rikki."

"We know who's *not* going to take the shot." Josh Elliott tipped his head toward Quinn. "You got yourself a bum shoulder, son. You're out of the running."

Quinn snorted. "I'm almost sure I still have better aim with my jacked-up shoulder than you do, Elliott. Hell, even skinny Miguel over there has you beat."

Miguel Estrada chucked a glove at Quinn. "Watch it. I may have dropped a few pounds, but I've got more reason than anyone here to make that shot count."

The door to the loft in the schloss a half mile away from Vlad's cottage burst open, and every last sniper reached for his weapon.

A woman with dark hair in a ponytail wedged her hands on her slim hips. "I'll make that decision when the time comes."

Quinn's jaw dropped. He'd had a vague picture of Ariel in his head, but this woman, whose face they all knew, wasn't it.

Alexei, the blunt Russian-American, voiced what was in all their heads. "You! Lauren West, the wife of Defense Secretary West."

"That's not who I am here." She crossed her arms and propped up the doorjamb with her shoulder. "I'm Ariel, and I'm still the leader of this task force."

Once they all got over the shock of Mrs. Shane West being the infamous Ariel, they dug in to discuss their plans.

They wouldn't all be stationed in this hunting lodge. They had visibility of Vlad's schloss from a few well-hidden treetops and a museum that would be closed to the public tomorrow.

Ariel instructed Austin to keep tabs on Rikki and to notify her immediately if it looked like Rikki was not headed in their direction.

Quinn clamped a fist against the knots in his gut. He had to be right about the location of this meeting. It made too much sense. It synced up with Ariel's belief that the meeting would be in this forest.

His gaze tracked to the vibrant brunette giving orders as well as or better than her husband ever did, and Shane West was one of them—a retired navy SEAL sniper. How had she known? What connection did she have with Vlad? Her husband had come up against him a few times, but nothing like how the team in this room had.

A few hours later, after a meal and talk about the assignments that had led them all to this forest on this night, Quinn's teammates began scattering again—this time to take down a terrorist who had threatened them all and the ones they loved.

THE NEXT MORNING, Quinn peeled a banana and made it his breakfast. He had stayed in the schloss with Ariel, the only two who had buddied up, and for the hundredth time he cursed the gunshot wound in his shoulder. But if he thought his close proximity to Ariel would get her to open up, he couldn't be more wrong.

Which one of them would Ariel choose for the honor? All of them were at the top of their game, even Miguel after his time in captivity. Alexei could be a hothead, but not in a sniper situation, and Slade was laid-back enough to step away and let others take credit.

He and Josh had the most experience, but given his current condition, it might fall to Josh Elliott to take out their nemesis.

It was anyone's guess at this point, and Ariel kept her lips sealed.

The radio crackled, and Austin's cowboy twang came over the airwaves. "Our subject is on the move. Leaving the hotel."

Quinn tossed the banana peel in their make-shift trash bag and wiped his hands on his jeans. He shouldn't have eaten anything. His stomach churned.

Ariel studied him through narrowed eyes. "Don't worry about Rikki. She can handle herself."

"I know that, but if this isn't the meeting place, I screwed up royally and we'll have to scramble to catch up to them."

"You didn't screw up, Quinn. This is it."

He ran his tongue along his teeth. "How can you be so sure? How did you know it would be Grunewald forest when Rikki mentioned Berlin?"

Fire sparked from her dark eyes, and her nostrils flared, giving her a completely different appearance from the sophisticated, put-together lady of Washington. "You're not the only one who knows Vlad."

Quinn's brain whirred for the best response to get Ariel to open up, but Austin's voice interrupted him.

"They're on the autobahn, leaving the city."

The knots returned to Quinn's gut, and his shoulder throbbed. A jumbled prayer ran through his head that Rikki would head straight to the schloss, that she'd be safe, that Bella would be safe.

Austin's voice filled the room. "Headed this way. On track. The subject is on track."

The others hooted and whooped it up, but Quinn silently thanked God as his gaze met Ariel's.

Throughout the morning, strangers had wandered into the forest and along the lake, and the team had ID'd them as operatives for Vlad. They clearly had no clue that they were already surrounded by a team of navy SEAL snipers and a support group whose sole purpose over the past year had been to neutralize Vlad and his terrorist network.

None of them knew what Vlad looked like. He'd changed his appearance like a chameleon in every fuzzy, vague photo they had of him. But he'd be the one meeting with Dawson and Rikki. There would be no question about that, so they had to wait. They couldn't just start taking down people as they got out of cars or made their way to Vlad's hunting lodge, giving him a heads-up.

After the tense waiting of the morning, everything started unfolding faster than Quinn had anticipated.

Ariel started spitting out directions in the military

manner she must've learned from her husband, the secretary. She had Quinn zeroing in on the car carrying Rikki and Dawson.

He'd had some painkiller injected directly into his shoulder, and the numbness prevented him from even feeling the heft of his rifle resting there. The car pulled up on the gravel drive of the schloss, and Rikki stepped out.

For the second time in less than two years, Quinn lined her up in his scope. He whispered. "C'mon, Buttercup. We're gonna do this."

Rikki threw back her head, laughing at some quip from Dawson, but Quinn could almost believe she'd heard his quiet entreaty.

Another car pulled up, and several men exited.

Quinn held his breath. The tension coming off Ariel stifled the air in the room.

She'd joined him at the window, her own rifle, a sleek, deadly model, hoisted and ready. How long had she trained for this?

As the group began moving toward the house, Rikki paused and shook hands with a tall man, the sun glinting off his clean-shaven head.

With rapid fire, Ariel gave them their targets. Josh had the man Rikki had just greeted. He must be Vlad. Lucky bastard.

Quinn had the driver as his target, but they had to assume he was armed as well and would pose a threat to Rikki and even Dawson once the shooting ended.

Ariel gave the countdown before the group could

even move inside. She must be sure of Vlad and that he wasn't waiting inside for them.

Three. Two. One.

Quinn felled his target and then swept his scope to the other fallen men. They'd left Dawson alive, and his mouth gaped in shock.

Then he reached for a weapon as Rikki backed away from him, and Quinn took his second shot.

Rikki stood amid the dead men, her face composed, her dark hair blowing in the breeze.

Slade, who'd been stationed in one of the trees, closest to the schloss, ran onto the scene and grabbed Rikki and pulled her away. Vlad could still have reinforcements nearby, but the head of the snake had been chopped off.

Josh cackled from the museum. "I got him, boys. I got that bald-headed bastard."

Ariel winked at Quinn. "No, you didn't, Elliott. Vlad was mine. He was always going to be mine."

Epilogue

Quinn held a sleeping Bella in the crook of his arm as he stood on the hotel room's balcony next to Miguel's son, Mikey, and RJ, the son of Josh's girl-friend, Gina.

RJ squirmed. "When are the fireworks?"

"Another half hour, buddy." Quinn patted his head.

Josh swept up the boy and put him on his shoulders. "You can watch from up here when they start."

Gina came up behind them and wrapped one arm around Josh's waist as she tugged on RJ's foot. "Patience. I'm going to get you and Mikey some more food."

Miguel scooped up Mikey. "You hungry?"

Jennifer, Miguel's wife, hovered next to both of them. "I think he's been stuffing his face with beignets all day. You need to eat something, too, doesn't he, Quinn?"

Miguel rolled his eyes at Quinn. "She thinks I'm gonna break."

Quinn slugged Miguel in the arm. "This guy's unbreakable."

He cuddled Bella against his shoulder and strolled into the hotel suite where the childless couples had gathered, drinking more than the parents and anticipating the fireworks less.

Austin's girlfriend, Sophia, sat on the arm of his chair, excitedly making a point by grabbing his arm, the diamond in the side of her nose catching the light.

Austin shrugged. "I think that's a good idea, Sophia."

Quinn grinned and elbowed Slade. "The kid might be young, but he catches on quickly."

Slade winked. "I taught him everything he knows about women."

"I don't think there's enough time in the world for that." He pointed at Slade's girlfriend, Nicole, deep in discussion with Alexei. "What are those two cooking up?"

"The mad Russian has Nicole convinced that she needs to do a documentary film on the crime families of Russia."

"Do you want me to stop him?"

"Nicole will do exactly what she wants, but Alexei's girl, Britt, can keep him in line." Slade waved at Britt, and she shrugged, a smile curving her lips, as she stroked Alexei's hair. "She even has Alexei on board for adopting the orphaned baby of his worst enemy."

Slade cranked his head from side to side. "Did you invite Ariel, or should I say, Mrs. West?"

"I did invite her, but she and the secretary are at

the White House for the fireworks." Quinn checked his watch. "Probably already saw them."

"Did Rikki ever tell you how or why Ariel knew Vlad?"

Rikki swooped in on them and kissed the bottom of Bella's foot. "That's Ariel's business."

Slade raised his eyebrows. "But you know."

"I'm a CIA agent, sailor." Rikki drew her fingertip across the seam of her lips.

Slade laughed and crouched beside his sleek, polished girlfriend as she grabbed his hand and began to tell him about her new project in Russia.

Rikki patted the bandage on Quinn's shoulder. "Feeling okay?"

"It aches. My doctor was not happy when I told him about that shot I got that allowed me to hoist my rifle."

"But you nailed your target…and I'm glad you did."

"Dawson was going for a gun, Rikki. He was going to kill you for betraying him."

"I know that." She kissed his shoulder. "You don't have to defend yourself. I don't think Belinda Dawson was too upset by the turn of events, either. The CIA already talked to her, and they're going light on her."

"What about my buddy Jeff? Did Ariel tell you what was going on in New Orleans?"

"Purely bad luck. That *was* the Agency on his tail. They noted his suspicious movements and were tracking him. Seems after that Rikki Taylor turned, the CIA got jumpy."

"Can you blame them?" He tugged on a lock of her red hair. "Did you know which one was Vlad before we opened fire and Ariel killed him?"

"No. I was being introduced around. David never gave away Vlad's identity. I don't think I would've ever known. Each of those men at the schloss planned to join us for the meeting, so I never would've known which one was Vlad." She shook her head. "I still can't believe David was stupid enough to put details of Vlad's hideaway in his book. I'm sure he never told Vlad about that."

"Like I said, hubris. Dawson was the only one who'd come close enough to Vlad, outside of Vlad's inner circle, who even knew he had that hunting lodge by the lake."

"Tobias Bauer. His name is not Vlad." Alexei stood up and uttered some oath in Russian. "Let's not give him that power anymore."

Nicole asked, "But who was he exactly? Can you tell us that?"

Quinn glanced at Josh and shrugged. "The intelligence agencies are still figuring that out, but we know he was a child of about ten in East Germany when the Berlin Wall fell. He and his mother moved to the more prosperous cities of West Germany during the reunification, but she died soon after and Toby, as he was called, took to the streets—stealing, hustling, getting in trouble with the authorities."

Austin's girlfriend slid into his lap and said, "He had my friend killed. How did he become a terrorist?"

"And where did he learn how to shoot?" Jennifer,

Miguel's wife, shooed the kids back onto the balcony with Rikki's mother and stepfather.

Slade answered, "He learned how to shoot in the forest. He became an excellent marksman and started hiring himself out as a mercenary."

"And a master of disguise." Miguel put his arm around his wife. "I may have even seen him when I was held in those caves. Nobody really knew what he looked like."

"Except Ariel." Austin cleared his throat and glanced at Rikki.

"As more is discovered about him, his terrorist network will be dismantled." Josh raised his glass. "To the fall of Tobias Bauer and the protection of innocents everywhere."

A boom echoed from outside and RJ dashed into the room from the balcony. "The fireworks. The fireworks."

Quinn tucked his sleeping daughter into a bassinet and took Rikki's hand. She squeezed his hand and they kissed before joining everyone on the balcony.

While holding on to the woman he loved, Quinn watched the exploding colors reflected in the faces of his teammates. One by one, he met their eyes and nodded, a silent affirmation among them all that they'd do anything to protect the people gathered here and to protect the red, white and blue.

* * * * *

COMING NEXT MONTH FROM

⊞ HARLEQUIN®

INTRIGUE

Available March 20, 2018

#1773 ROUGHSHOD JUSTICE
Blue River Ranch • by Delores Fossen
It's been two years since Texas Ranger Jameson Beckett has seen
Kelly Stockwell. Now she's crashed back into his life with a toddler and no
memory of their once-intense relationship.

#1774 SUDDEN SETUP
Crisis: Cattle Barge • by Barb Han
Ella Butler wasn't expecting rescue in the form of Holden Crawford, a
perfect stranger. But will his protection be enough to save her from ruthless
killers, let alone absolve him of his own dark past?

#1775 DROPPING THE HAMMER
The Kavanaughs • by Joanna Wayne
After a brutal kidnapping, Rachel Maxwell isn't sure she's still the powerful
attorney she once was. Cowboy Luke Dawkins is also trying to escape a
troubled past, and maybe they can remind each other what true strength—
and love—looks like.

#1776 DESPERATE STRANGERS
by Carla Cassidy
Julie Peterson's amnesia gives Nick Simon the perfect alibi—after all, she
doesn't realize that she only just met her "fiancé" at the scene of a crime.
But can she trust Nick as her only protector when a dangerous killer draws
close?

#1777 TRIBAL BLOOD
Apache Protectors: Wolf Den • by Jenna Kernan
His time with the marines left him speechless with nightmares, but when
pregnant Kasey Doka escapes a surrogacy ring and seeks out his help,
Colt Redhorse feels something between them that goes deeper than words.

#1778 FEDERAL AGENT UNDER FIRE
Protectors of Cade County • by Julie Anne Lindsey
For years FBI agent Blake Garrett has obsessed over a serial killer...a killer
who has now become obsessed with the one woman to escape with her
life—Melissa Lane. Can Blake protect her without his fixation clouding his
judgment?

Get 2 Free Books,
Plus 2 Free Gifts—
just for trying the Reader Service!

I N T R I G U E

SPECIAL EXCERPT FROM

> *A killer stole her voice. Now she's ready to take it back.*
> *Don't miss the next chilling installment in the*
> ***SHADES OF DEATH** series*
> *from USA TODAY bestselling author Debra Webb.*

Turn the page for a sneak peek from
THE LONGEST SILENCE
by ***Debra Webb**, coming March 2018.*

New York Times *bestselling author Sandra Brown*
calls it "a gripping read."

The phone wouldn't stop ringing. The annoying sound echoed off the dingy walls of the tiny one-room apartment.

Joanna Guthrie chewed her thumbnail as she stared at the damned cell phone. Three people had this number: her boss, a research analyst she occasionally worked with and Ellen. If it was work, the caller would simply leave a message, but it wasn't work—it was Ellen.

Jo's foot started to tap so she stood and paced the floor. "Not answering."

Why should she answer? The calls came about three or four times a year and they were always the same. Ellen would complain about her life and her husband and her kids. She would bemoan the hand fate had dealt her. She would never be whole. Nothing she attempted fixed her. Not the shrinks or the meditation or the yoga or any of the other crazier shit she'd tried, like cocaine, and certainly not the alcohol.

The ringing stopped.

Jo stared at the phone. Two minutes tops and it would start that fucking ringing again. She closed her eyes and exhaled a measure of the frustration always generated by calls from Ellen. Guilt immediately took its place. No matter the reason, whenever Ellen called Jo always wound up feeling guilty whether she answered the damned phone or not. A voice mail carried the same guilt-generating effect.

"Not my fault." She paced the room like a freshly incarcerated criminal on the front end of a life sentence.

Ellen had chosen her own path. She'd made the decision to pretend to be normal. Dared to marry and to have children. Jo shook her head. How the hell could she do that after what they'd gone through—what they'd done? Now the woman spent every minute of every day terrified that she would somehow disappoint her family or that something bad would happen to them because of her. Or, worse, that someone would discover her secret—their secret.

Deep breath. "Not my problem."

Jo had made the smarter choice. She'd cut ties with her family and friends. No boyfriends, much less husbands. No kids for damned sure. If she wanted sexual release she either took care of it herself or she picked up a soldier from one of the clubs in Killeen. She didn't go to church; she didn't live in the same town for more than a year. She never shared her history with anyone. Not that there was anything in her past that would give anyone reason to suspect the truth, but she hated the looks of sympathy, the questions.

The past was over and done. Dragging it into the present would not change what was done.

She had boundaries. Boundaries to protect herself. She never wasted time making small talk, much less friends. Besides, she wasn't in one place long enough for anyone to notice or to care. Since her employer was an online newspaper, she rarely had to interact face-to-face with anyone. In fact, she and the boss had never met in person and he was the closest thing to a friend she had.

Whatever that made her, Jo didn't care.

Hysterical laughter bubbled into her throat. Even the IRS didn't have her address. She used the newspaper's address for anything permanent. Her boss faxed her whatever official-looking mail he received, and then shredded it. He never asked why. Jo supposed he understood somehow.

She recognized her behavior for what it was—paranoia. Plain and simple. Six years back she'd noticed one of those health fairs in the town where she'd lived. Probably not the most scientific or advanced technology since it was held in a school cafeteria. Still, she'd been desperate to ensure nothing had been implanted in her body—like some sort of tracking device—so she'd scraped up enough money to pay for a full-body scan. Actually, she'd been short fifty bucks but the tech had accepted a quick fuck in exchange. After all that trouble he'd found nothing. Ultimately that was a good thing but it had pissed her off at the time.

A ring vibrated the air in the room.

Enough. Jo snatched up the phone. "What do you want, Ellen?"

The silence on the other end sent a surge of oily black uncertainty snaking around her heart. When she would have ended the call, words tumbled across the dead air.

"This is Ellen's husband."

A new level of doubt nudged at Jo. "Art?"

She had no idea how she'd remembered the man's name. Personal details were something else she had obliterated from her life. Distance and anonymity were her only real friends now.

Now? She almost laughed out loud at her vast understatement. Eighteen years. She'd left any semblance of a normal life behind eighteen years ago. Jesus Christ, had it only been eighteen?

Don't miss
THE LONGEST SILENCE,
available March 2018 wherever
MIRA® Books and ebooks are sold.

www.Harlequin.com

MDWEXP1017

Need an adrenaline rush from nail-biting tales (and irresistible males)?

Check out **Harlequin® Intrigue®** and **Harlequin® Romantic Suspense** books!

New books available every month!

CONNECT WITH US AT:

Harlequin.com/Community

 Facebook.com/HarlequinBooks

 Twitter.com/HarlequinBooks

 Instagram.com/HarlequinBooks

 Pinterest.com/HarlequinBooks

ReaderService.com

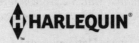

ROMANCE WHEN YOU NEED IT

SGENRE2017